LAURA GERINGER

SILVERPOINT

 A Charlotte Zolotow Book

An Imprint of HarperCollins*Publishers*

Thanks to Tony and to Charlotte for allowing
me the time to write this book and for believing
it would really be a book someday. And thanks to
Joanna for giving me a quiet place in which to
work and support above and beyond the call of
friendship.

L.G.

Grateful acknowledgement is made for permission
to reprint an excerpt from *The Town Beyond the
Wall* © 1964 by Elie Wiesel.

SILVERPOINT
Copyright © 1991 by Laura Geringer
All rights reserved. No part of this book may be used or
reproduced in any manner whatsoever without written
permission except in the case of brief quotations embodied in
critical articles and reviews. Printed in the United States of
America. For information address HarperCollins Children's
Books, a division of HarperCollins Publishers, 10 East 53rd
Street, New York, NY 10022.
Typography by Anahid Hamparian
1 2 3 4 5 6 7 8 9 10
First Edition

Library of Congress Cataloging-in-Publication Data
Geringer, Laura.
    Silverpoint / by Laura Geringer.
        p.   cm.
    "A Charlotte Zolotow book."
    Summary: On the eve of her twelfth birthday, Cora convinces
herself that the father she has never known is on his way to see
her.
    ISBN 0-06-023849-6. — ISBN 0-06-023850-X (lib. bdg.)
    [1. Fathers and daughters—Fiction.]   I. Title.
PZ7.G296Si   1991   91-6648
[Fic]—dc20   CIP
                                                                          AC

For Anya

CONTENTS

SILVERPOINT

1
THE BIRTHDAY

While waiting for her mother to come home from work, Cora liked to talk to the crackers in her soup. Sitting alone at the kitchen table, she chose her favorites carefully and let them float. The others she bullied with her spoon, encouraging them to spread into sog. As long as they kept their shape, they were safe. But once they started to go soft, she would begin to explain why their time was up. "Oysterettes, I greet you; and now I will eat you," she would say ceremoniously. And she would hold them under the hot broth, holding her breath all the while.

But the day before her twelfth birthday, Cora looked at the crackers and began to cry. "You dumb things," she sobbed, "you never *answer* me!" She stalked into the living room, marching directly up to last year's birthday present from her mother—a smiling wooden bear, hand carved in some foreign country—and for no reason at all pulled off its head.

That night at dinner, her mother didn't mention Cora's birthday. She talked on and on about her job at school and then about the news.

Cora wasn't interested. "Did you know some girl in Iowa changed her name to Honey Graham in order to win first prize in a cookie contest?" she asked.

"No, I didn't," said her mother.

"*That's* news!" said Cora, and left the table, heading for her room.

Wearily, she trudged over to her bed and sank down on the pillow. She had been thinking all month about what she wanted for her birthday. Her friend Charley had a turtle, and for a while she thought she would ask her mother to get her one too. But Charley spent a lot of time tracking and catching live bugs in a Band-Aid box, and she wasn't certain she was committed enough for that. She had liked finding the praying mantis and capturing it. They hadn't fed it to the turtle—just watched it praying and let it go. But most often, Charley would spend hours in the park and return with a few houseflies. Cora had begun turning down his invitations to insect safaris now that it was hot. It was boring standing around in the bushes, watching for signs of a slow-moving beetle. She had better things to do.

Charley never bought Cora a birthday present in a store. He just picked out something he thought she would like from what was already in his house. But other than the turtle, the only thing she really liked in Charley's house these days was a twin set of tiny dolls made out of bullets—one balancing a jug on her head, the other lifting her lead skirt. They were very heavy when Cora held them in her hand. Charley said they were made from the bullets that had killed his father. One had been shot into his leg; the other had pierced his heart.

Charley's story wasn't too clear, and Cora didn't know whether to believe him or not. But she wished whatever it was that had caused her own father to leave when she was a baby could be made into dull little pellets, solid like that, so she could finger them and feel their weight.

Cora pulled off her clothes and put on her pajamas, though it was still much too early to go to sleep. Most kids had parties for their birthdays. But her mother didn't like parties and neither did Charley, so there was no one to invite.

Every birthday it was the same. She waited for her father to show up. Not that she would recognize him if he did. Her mother hadn't saved any photographs, though she *had* saved a few mementos.

On the wall near her desk, Cora had hung her father's old ties, a colorful group including several with corny patterns of barnyard animals—pigs and horses and cows. And then there was his bamboo birdcage. Her mother said he had never kept a bird in it, but had just liked the way it looked. Wedged into one of the slats, Cora had once discovered a slip of paper with his name scrawled across it like the fortune in a Chinese cookie: *Nikos Pavlides.* She had folded it into a tiny square and hidden it deep in her jewelry box, inside the velvet pouch where she kept her good luck thunderbird pin from Teepee Town and her birthstone ring. Often, she took it out and looked at it again, studying the tight shape and slant of his signature.

Cora stared up at the ceiling and sighed. He could have at least written her a letter before he disappeared. She was only a few cells at the time, but he must have known she would get bigger and be able to read someday. Why hadn't he thought to leave her a message, to be opened on her twelfth birthday?

The third and last souvenir of her dad was dangling from a hook above her pillow. It was an odd bunch of broken stuff he had put together as a joke just before he left—a pair of motorcycle goggles with one lens missing, a plastic watch with a mermaid swimming clockwise (though by now she had stopped swimming), a gold pencil sharpener, and a miniature ceramic dog that could pop out of its kennel but was now stuck half in and half out—all tied to a twisted leather thong. On windy nights, the thing did a monotonous dance, casting dim shadows onto the ceiling. But there were no shadows tonight, and no hint of a breeze.

Cora sat up suddenly and looked out the window. The round globe of her bedside lamp appeared in the pane, a ghost of itself. She remembered how she used to think there was a whole world hovering somewhere between the inside of their home and the park outside, before she learned about reflections in glass. She had thought perhaps her father lived in *that* place and was watching her at night.

In fact, he lived in Greece—if he hadn't moved by now. He had gone there for what was supposed to have been a brief visit and had been drafted into the Greek army. Before his term of service was over, he had decided not to return.

Cora yawned, and slid down under the covers. Her mother always said her father was a little crazy, but Cora didn't believe her. In fact, sometimes

Cora thought her mother was the crazy one.

Like the time Cora woke at three in the morning, to find her mother busy at the kitchen table, pasting news clippings neatly into a scrapbook. They were all about rescues. A WOMAN LOST FOR DAYS ON THE SLOPES OF A FOUR-THOUSAND-FOOT MOUNTAIN IN OREGON KEPT HERSELF ALIVE BY EATING BERRIES. AN OLD MAN FOUND IN A TOOLSHED HAD BEEN HELD THERE AGAINST HIS WILL FOR SEVEN YEARS.

Her mother had worn no robe that night. Shivering in her nylon nightgown, she had whispered, "Maybe someone will rescue *us*," and her long breasts had looked to Cora like twin sad faces, veiled in lace.

"Do we need to be rescued?" Cora had asked, whispering too.

Later, she wondered if she had dreamed the whole thing or if it had really happened.

Cora wrapped the sheet tightly around herself until, lying rigidly on her back, her arms at her sides, she felt like a sewing needle in a half-finished hem. Traffic rumbled past, and she counted the reflections of truck windows traveling across the wall and across her father's neckties. She wondered drowsily if her father was listening to trucks go past *his* window, or if he lived in a city at all. She wondered if he still wore ties with animals on them and if he missed his birdcage. She wondered what *he* would have given her for her birthday, and if he knew it was her birthday tomorrow, or if he had forgotten the date long ago.

2
EUROPA

That night, Cora dreamed she was on her way to Greece in an ocean liner to find her father. He had not invited her, but somehow she knew it was time to go look for him.

The captain of the ship was a bald man in a white suit. Soothed by the rocking of the waves as the big boat headed toward Greece, Cora watched his smooth head reflecting little dancing streaks of sunlight like a movie screen.

They landed on an island called Kharonia. Cora went looking for an inn, trudging toward a knot of stunted, whitewashed buildings. A small girl with a basket rode by astride a donkey. She smelled strongly of shoe polish. She called hello to Cora in English and said her name was Baubo.

Cora asked if Baubo knew a place where a traveler could spend the night. The girl told her there were no hotels, but she offered Cora a fig from her basket and asked if she would like to come home with her.

"I'm looking for my father," Cora said, as they walked through the town. "Do you know him? His name is Nikos."

"I know a few men named Nikos," said the girl. "My own father's name was Nikos. He died when I was a baby."

"My best friend Charley's father died too," said Cora. "He was a soldier, I think."

"How do you know *your* father isn't dead?" asked the girl.

The two girls fell silent, walking along side by side until they came to a small house. A woman ran out, shooing a flock of geese into the yard. She wore a threadbare black blouse, but Cora could see it had once been a splashy print of large flowers that still showed through the dark dye. Her face was worried but friendly, and she ushered them into a tiny kitchen, where she gave Cora a glass of cool water and a spoonful of white taffy.

Cora drank gratefully, and sucked the sweet candy as Baubo rattled on in Greek. Her mother made little clucks of interest and understanding, once touching Cora's shoulder and gazing deeply into her eyes.

In a corner, a skinny black cat poked portions of itself out from under a table—first its paw, then its head, then its tail. The girl teased it with a branch of brown berries.

Cora suddenly felt so tired, she let her head sink down on the table. She wondered absently how to say "I'm sleepy" in Greek. "I'll have to learn Greek," she thought, yawning.

The woman led Cora to a pretty room, painted peacock blue, with a heart-shaped mirror over a clean cot, a spluttering lantern, and a love seat embroidered with doves. "Good night," she said in English, and shut the door.

A calendar print of Europa and the Bull hung on the wall, and Cora went up close to it, studying the scene. She had been learning about Greek mythology in school, and Europa was her favorite story.

She tried to imagine the kidnapping: the graceful Europa with her friends, playing in a field of flowers beside her father's seaside palace. The girls weaving garlands for the gods. All at once, a herd of cattle moving silently toward them across the grass. And in the center, a beautiful white bull, his horns gleaming like gold. Zeus in disguise!

Kneeling at Europa's feet, he looks at her longingly with big, soft brown eyes. She laughs and claps her hands, then climbs upon his broad back. The beast rushes away toward the ocean, and she trembles as they plunge into the waves. But to her surprise, not a drop of spray touches her purple robe as it billows out behind her like a sail. Then the sea sprites, rising up out of the water, blow a blast as jolly as wedding bells on a giant conch shell and follow the pair all the way to Crete, where Zeus reveals himself and tells Europa he loves her.

But was Europa really happy after that? Cora asked herself. Was she still happy after she had her first child and the Bull was no longer there very much? That was the question none of the books answered. There were lots of gods showing up in disguise and going away again. But what about their wives, left all alone in a mist? Were they glad they had been chosen? Or were they angry, like her mother?

"This is not a dream anymore," thought Cora, and she woke, so annoyed at herself for ending the dream before she found her father that she began to cry.

"It's a dream, only a dream," came her mother's voice. "Wake up, Cora—it's all right." Suddenly, her mother was there, holding her close.

Cora, still weeping, shut her eyes tight, trying to

go back to her little blue room in the Greek village. But her mother smelled so good, and spoke so softly, that Cora let the dream go and just rested there in her mother's arms like a baby.

3
THE ANGEL

Cora loved her mother in the middle of the night. She had a theory. When her father left, she guessed, her mother had split into two—the day mother and the night mother. The night mother was the way she must have been before he left—kind of vague and dreamy and soft. The night mother hugged her when she woke from a dream or just couldn't sleep. But the day mother was always a little rushed and tense.

Cora told her theory to Charley after school on their way to the park the next day. He thought she was probably right. He said he could remember *his* mother before his dad was killed and she was different. She still hugged him a lot day *and* night, he said. But now she was usually in a hurry. She never just sat around anymore and let him talk. She was the one who talked, always telling him what to do, and she didn't like to play games like

Cootie anymore either.

"We can play Cootie at my house later," Cora promised him. "But we have to stop at the library first. I have to learn Greek." Then she told him about her dream. "How am I ever going to find my father if I can't even speak the language?" she concluded urgently. "Maybe you should learn Greek too, Charley. Then nobody would understand what we were saying."

"Nobody understands that anyway," he said, smiling.

Cora looked at Charley smiling at her, his white-blond hair curling all over his head like bleached leaves of lettuce. He had been her best friend since first grade. Their teacher that year, Miss Bousefield, had been a professional dancer and she had wanted all her students to dance. Her clothes were cream-colored and as filmy as a fly's wings. And she would sit very straight at a vast black piano as dusty light from the barred window filtered through her blouse.

"Imagine the moon, children," she would sing out, waving her thin arms wildly in a circle. "Imagine the sun. Think of the earth moving in a circle around the sun. Think round, children, think round and turn, turn, turn like little tops. Come, little planets, turn. Don't be shy; come closer.

Come make a heavenly arc around me, closer, closer, closer, that's right."

"What am I going to *do?*" Charley had whispered that first day, clutching onto Cora's arm. "I can't dance." She had taken his hand, and they had become partners, pretending to be planets and prancing horses and slow-moving elephants with long, graceful trunks. After school, Charley imitated Miss Bousefield (Prance! Prance! Step, step, step—lift those legs, lift them higher!). They would go to the park together and practice new dances like the Cockroach Waltz, leaping around and laughing so hard their sides hurt.

Today, they were heading for the park, but not to dance.

"Some people watch birds or gorillas in the jungle and write down what they see," Cora had explained when her mother had grounded her for a week after coming across the notebook in which she and Charley recorded their daily findings. "We watch people in the park. And we write down what *we* see. What's wrong with that?"

But she had to admit, it made for strange reading if you browsed through. It wasn't just anyone they watched. It was the crazies, like the Mushroom and Miss Nancy. She had started the game, but it was Charley who had introduced the scientific diary, with a pencil tied to the binding and dated observations:

May 16 THE MUSHROOM sits in the cafeteria near the playground and orders things from kids going by. "A large glass of gullymongus, please," he says. "A couple of palamas and a side order of croptis—if it's fresh." The kids don't pay much attention to him, and sometimes he gets mad. "You got borely in your ears or what?" he shouts. "I'd like one of those dolpatches you got there and a nice hot cup of sifrak."

We call him the Mushroom because he looks like one. He has a black suitcase but he never opens it. Question: What's in his suitcase?

June 1 MISS NANCY sits on a bench and feeds the pigeons bread and dried figs. She says the fruit of temptation in the Bible was a fig, not an apple. She says, "Greed is the worst of the seven sins."

Last time, she told us a story about a fisherman. His name was Ibrahim Mohammed Karkour. He stood in the Nile and spread his net. Then he felt a fish caught under each foot. He bent down and grabbed one fish and put it between his teeth before he dived for the other. The first fish got into his throat and drowned him. And that was the end of Ibrahim Mohammed Karkour. All because he was greedy and wanted two fish instead of one.

Today, Miss Nancy told us that she swallows things: keys, rosary beads, pennies, a nail file once in a while, and tweezers. She never chokes, though. We asked her if it hurt to swallow things. She said it tickled. "If you can tickle yourself, you can always laugh. Remember that," she said. Question: Why does she like pigeons so much?

Now that her mother had read the notebook, Cora had to be more careful about her conversations with Charley on the phone. Cora had grudgingly promised her mother not to talk with any more crazies. But she hadn't told Charley about the promise, and she knew that she wouldn't be able to keep her word, at least not right away. The talks were just too interesting, and she was angry at her mother for snooping. Anyway, she felt safe with Charley. He would never let anything bad happen to her, no matter what.

As they detoured down Dyckman Street toward the library, Cora scanned the block. The coast looked disappointingly clear. The park was always the best scouting grounds for crazies. But sometimes, she and Charley struck gold at the library, in the reading room or, in nice weather, on the steps.

They passed the bakery, and Cora peered through the glass at the trio of ladies working behind the counter. They were sisters, all very round with chunky fingers, but their hands moved swiftly, tying boxes and boxes of cakes together with white string. Next door, the cat dozed in the window of Mr. Popper's butcher shop. As customers came in, clouds of dust rose in the air, dulling the whine of grinding knives.

"The whooping crane at the San Diego zoo laid an egg yesterday. Isn't that great?" Charley announced as they climbed the library steps.

"Yeah," said Cora, but she wasn't in the mood for one of Charley's informative talks on vanishing species.

As they entered the cool, dimly lit reading room, Cora saw her favorite librarian, Flora, at her post behind the front desk. Usually, she stood around and joked with Flora about how their names rhymed and quizzed her about the books on display to make sure Flora was keeping up with her reading. But today, Cora just waved and eyed the shelves, fidgeting. Charley motioned her over to a table. She pulled away from him. "I'll meet you by the desk," she whispered, making a beeline for the section on foreign languages.

She knelt down and picked out all the Greek books, stacking them neatly on the floor. There were just a few. Two were entirely in Greek, and she put those back. One was the bilingual text of a play called *Lysistrata,* which looked too difficult, so she replaced that one too. *Teach Yourself Greek*—this was it! She leafed through the yellowed pages. "Lilika eats roast lamb," she read. She turned the page. "The street, of the street, to the street, street. The field, of the field, to the field, field." It was like one of her jump-rope chants. And there were little black-and-white pictures—an ear, an eye, a hand. A bunch of grapes. And farther along—an airplane, a bicycle. Ah, here she was getting somewhere at last—an ocean liner, like the one in her dream. "Please speak slowly." *That* would be useful. And then, there it was, right in the middle of the page:

"Where is your father?"

Cora was just checking out her book when Charley's head poked out from behind a pillar. He had a thick encyclopedia of magic tricks under his arm. "Quick," he said, grabbing her hand and directing her toward the exit.

"What's the hurry? We just got here," Cora protested, letting herself be pulled along. They came to an abrupt halt by the door.

Sitting in the sun on a dirty box was an old man wearing a big-brimmed paper hat shaped like a figure eight and white evening gloves. He was turning the *New York Times* crossword puzzle, square by square, into a shimmering rainbow with a fistful of crayons. Propped against his cardboard seat stood a plastic harp, a torn shopping bag, and a beggar's cup that glared in the strong light. But what made Cora step back and blink were the man's six-foot silver wings!

"I've been an angel two weeks now," he said when he noticed them watching. And he tore into his newspaper, throwing bits to the breeze.

Cora caught her breath. An angel. But he looked more like a baby monkey than an angel, his reddened eyes round and bold as he studied them.

"I'm just a stand-in, a decoy till the real ones come," he said, as if reading Cora's thoughts. He let more confetti fly. Cora shaded her eyes and stared as one large piece clung to him, fluttering against his chest. Then he leaned toward her conspiratorially. "My first wife was nuts," he observed. "So was my second. What's your name? You newlyweds?"

"I'm Cora," she answered. "And this is Charley. We're not newlyweds, we're kids."

"Ahhhhh." He nodded. "Cora . . . Cora."

He pulled a Coca-Cola bottle from his tattered bag. It was filled with clear liquid and he took a sip, eyeing her. "What'd you say your name was? Starts with C, right?"

His lids trembled as if their weight had increased and the lines in his face seemed to deepen into troughs. He pointed to Charley's magic book. "Give it up, son," he said. "I was a magician once. Nah, give it up."

He dipped into his shopping bag again, and three bright plastic balls appeared in his hand. "Fine leather," he confided. "The best—passed on to me by the great So-and-So, master of the Egg Bag. Y'know that trick?"

He foraged in his bag again and produced a forked branch, waving it in the air. "Separates a man from his shadow," he explained. "And last but not least . . ." He reached in one more time and brought out a toy rabbit, with a key in its side. When he turned the key, the thing started to play "Here Comes Peter Cottontail."

"Well," he said apologetically, "the live ones eat too much." And he shrugged, putting his props away.

"How did you become a magician?" asked Charley skeptically.

"Bad luck," said the angel, winking. "Called myself the Amazing Sealini for a while and made a sea lion disappear. Yeah, a real sea lion. Didn't own her of course, just rented her. Bingo was her name, like the dog song. But poor Bingo would bark whenever she was supposed to be out of sight. Or she'd start rocking like she was saying her prayers. 'Why not hypnotize her?' I thought. Then she'd do what she was supposed to do. So I learned the hypnotizing business. Trouble is, I liked hypnotizing better than magic. Tried it on people too, and my wife, she didn't like it. Said she married a waiter, not a hypnotist. No, not a magician either.

"One day, whadya know, but I found her wedding dress, size nine, tossed over a lampshade and written on it in black ink: 'Don't blame yourself. Love, C.' with a little heart next to the Love. C for Claire, her name was Claire. And she was gone." Tears spilled down the angel's cheeks. He dabbed at them with a scrap of newspaper. "Think it's easy to love someone when they leave you?" he asked, staring at Cora.

Cora stepped closer to Charley. The angel pushed his hat back, worrying the fringe of dry hair that framed his face. "You know, most of life is avoiding pain," he said. "Think about it. You shine a light on an amoeba, and it moves away. You pull a dog's ears, and it runs. So many different kinds of pain: sharp, dull, welcome and not-so-welcome— you name it." He closed his eyes. "I don't know what kind of pain you'd call this," he said, placing his hand over his heart.

Cora stood riveted to the spot. She turned to Charley, who was watching her. "Let's go," he whispered.

She shook her head violently. Angels were the messengers of the gods. This one seemed crazy. But suppose he had been sent to find her? What if he had come from Greece, all the way from Mount Olympus?

"Do you have any messages for me?" she asked after a moment's silence.

"Think it's easy to love someone when they leave you?" he asked again, his eyes still closed and his hand still over his heart.

Suddenly, Cora felt faint. Multicolored dots swam before her eyes as if someone had taken her picture with a flash. She wasn't dizzy, just sightless for a moment. And in that blind instant, she knew—her father was on his way. She would find him in her dream first. But soon after that, she would turn around, and there he would be—in real life. She was going to meet him face to face at last.

Think it's easy to love someone when they leave you? No, it wasn't easy, Cora thought. It wasn't easy at all.

4
SILVERPOINT

"Cora, your father is no god and no angel either," said her mother for the third time that morning. "Get that through your head."

They were packing a picnic lunch to take to the beach and, as usual, it was taking forever. Cora's mother was carefully wrapping four thick chicken sandwiches in so many layers, they would take hours to unwrap—first the waxed paper, then the tinfoil, crisscrossed with a cat's cradle of rubber bands and, finally, the plastic bag. It was sweltering in their tiny kitchen and Cora wished for the hundredth time that her mother wasn't so slow.

"How do you know he's not?" she argued, helping her mother stack the food into the backpack. "How can you be so sure?" Then, before her mother could answer, she added, "Will you hurry *up*?"

Her mother was just as pokey when they went

shopping together in the supermarket. She wouldn't simply take a pack of string beans out of the deep freeze and drop it in her cart like Charley's mom. Oh no. She had to pick each bean fresh, one by one by one. Some were too soft. Some had their ends broken off or they had brown spots. Sometimes Cora thought if *she* had been born a string bean, her mother would have passed her by.

"You never used to think about your father so much," her mother complained. "All of a sudden, you can't *stop* thinking about him. It's one thing to study Greek myths in school," she added, pouring lemonade into a thermos. "It's another to think you *are* one. If I'm Europa and your father's Zeus, what does that make you?"

"Cinderella. You're missing the whole point."

"The *point* is . . ." Her mother broke off, considering whether to go on. She shook her head.

"I know what you were going to tell me," Cora said, angry now. "That he's crazy, right? That last you heard he went and joined some crazy cult in the Greek mountains, right? That he walks on coals now—hot coals. And he teaches other crazies how to do it. *Right?*"

"That's right," said her mother sadly.

"Well, how do you *know?*" Cora asked again.

"Gods and angels do all kinds of crazy things to disguise themselves. We're studying all that now in school. And the Greek gods lived on a mountain, didn't they? So just how can you be so sure? And how can you be sure you're not crazy too? Maybe you are, did you ever think of that? And maybe it's okay to be crazy. I'm crazy. You're crazy. My father's crazy. We're just one big crazy . . ." She stopped, not trusting her voice. "Family," she added a moment later.

Cora's idea of heaven, her father's home away from home, wasn't actually the Greek Mount Olympus at all. It was Silverpoint, the Long Island beach club she went to with her mother when the weather turned warm. She remembered her first visit. At the gate, she had been given a rubber tag to wear around her wrist that allowed her entry into the private gallery of little gaily painted huts. She had never seen a cabana before—they were like dollhouses, only bigger.

Cora had taken an endless stroll down the hot wooden boardwalk, staring into each one, memorizing the details of every gaudy family setting, the families perfect and whole: *father mother child.* She had loved them all on sight, baking like cookies on their platform porches, under their pretty umbrellas.

Cora had walked to the very end of the row, and then back again, staring until her tongue stuck to the roof of her mouth. Burning in the heat, she had sat and watched them, reading and playing and sleeping peacefully. Some had painted their noses metallic white; some had their eyes firmly shut against the sun, their shaded heads turned toward the ocean. And some looked as if they were waiting for something, like Cora herself.

"I'm sorry Charley couldn't come today," said her mother, as they spread their blanket on the sand and anchored the corners with shoes. "Whatever happened to Zeffy? Isn't she your friend anymore?"

Cora snorted. Her mother didn't like to admit that Charley was Cora's only friend. Zeffy was just the girl next door. Cora hadn't seen her much since fourth grade, when every day she had clattered out to the courtyard with Zeffy's coveted two-wheeler. Zeffy had been too fat to ride it herself. Zeffy had changed a lot since those days, of course. She wasn't fat anymore. Last year, she had been Cora's archrival in the jump-rope tournament. But she would never be a friend.

Cora listened to the sound of the waves. The sun had gone in again. Charley wasn't with her today because they weren't speaking to one another. After their meeting with the angel, Charley had taken out their notebook and started to write just as if the angel had been any old crazy in the park. "*June 12 THE ANGEL . . .*" he had scribbled before Cora had ripped the pencil out of his hand.

Charley simply didn't understand how important that meeting had been to her. He didn't even understand why she was so angry. She had tried to explain, but he hadn't wanted to listen because she had already yelled at him about the notebook. Cora wished they had never started that notebook. It had only gotten her in trouble with her mother, and now with Charley too.

She yawned and stretched out on the blanket. Even if there was no sun, she could still try to relax.

Her mother was more relaxed than if it had been sunny. She was strange that way. Bad news, she said, usually struck without warning, a bolt out of the blue. So when skies were blue, she was always waiting for the disaster, like Chicken Licken.

Cora remembered her mother reading her that story over and over again. "'Oh Henny Penny,'" she would exclaim with great feeling in a high, scratchy voice, "'the sky is falling and I'm on my way to tell the king!'" And so on, through Cocky Locky and Ducky Lucky and Goosey Loosey and

Turkey Lurkey and finally Foxy Loxy, who made it all come true.

"This is too perfect," her mother would often say on a gorgeous day, looking around guardedly. And she would make Cora pack up early, seeking shelter from the odds.

But now that clouds were piling up on the horizon, and a stiff wind was blowing, her mother seemed content. Calmly, she sat on her folding chair, reading a book.

Cora was startled out of her reverie by a piercingly high voice.

"Mama Mama Mama."

The little girl coming toward them was holding tightly to her own mother's hand and walking very quickly, her pale face set in a concentrated frown. "Mama," she whined again. And she pointed to the ocean.

"You can't go swimming today, sweetie," said her mother. "It's going to rain. See, the black flag is out. That means a storm is coming . . . . Look at the clouds over there." She pointed to the sky. The woman's eyes were a startling shade of violet.

Cora suddenly recognized the pair and nudged her mother. "Don't look now," she warned. "There's Mona and baby Evelyn."

Her mother continued to read for a minute.

"Oh *no*," she said absently. "And it's getting cold, too."

"It's been getting cold for the last half hour," said Cora. "Where have *you* been?"

Her mother smiled apologetically and sighed, looking up from her book. "Listen to this," she said, holding her place on the page. "It has to do with what we were talking about before—about being crazy."

"Wait, I think they see us," Cora interrupted.

Mona lived in their building, on the sixth floor. Her husband was Mr. Popper, the butcher. Sometimes, on weekends, he would carry his daughter downstairs in his thick arms, singing in an echoing baritone, songs like "Button up your overcoat, when the wind blows free. Take good care of yourself, you belong to me." And Evelyn would just giggle like the spoiled silly baby she would always be.

As far as Cora was concerned, Evelyn's only saving grace was her spit bubbles. She could spin out giant rainbow ones, forever holding them on her slippery mouth and grinning at the same time, like a fish under water.

"MamaMamaMamaMamaMama!" Evelyn was shrieking now.

"What *is* it?" her mother demanded, shaking her

head as if to clear it.

"Baba."

The mother smiled, relieved. She slipped a bottle from her shoulder bag and held it up. It was empty. "Well, we'll get some milk for your baba right now," she said reassuringly. "The snack bar's over there, see?" Again, she pointed. But Evelyn began to wail.

"Mona, hi," Cora's mother called out, waving. "Do you want me to watch her while you get some milk?"

Mona looked vastly relieved as she guided Evelyn over to the blanket. Evelyn stopped crying but continued to whimper, putting her fingers in her mouth and studying Cora's mother. "Mommy's going to get you a nice baba," said Mona, backing away. "You be a good girl," she added. Then, calling over her shoulder as she hurried toward the refreshment stand, she yelled, "Thanks."

"Yeah, you're welcome," Cora mumbled, giving her mother a disgusted look. First the day had turned cloudy and too chilly for swimming and now *this*.

Her mother was making foolish crooning noises and doing a strange dance step with the baby, patting her on the back at the same time. "Shhh, shhhh, sweetie pie. You're okay, you're okay, everything is okay. Choo, choo, choo," she murmured. She was getting sand on the blanket. Cora looked around to be sure no one was watching.

"What a crybaby," she commented.

But her mother looked blissful and continued to croon, shifting from foot to foot.

"I used to do this with you twenty-four hours a day," she said, pausing for a moment. "You cried *all* the time." Then she swung back into her routine and even started to sing, "I love you a bushel and a peck, a bushel and a peck and a hug around the neck, a doodle doodle doo, a doodle doodle doo . . . I love you." And she hugged Evelyn. The baby smiled.

"Did you sing that song to *me*?" asked Cora, turning red.

"It was one of your favorites," said her mother.

"Did I really cry so much?"

"Oh yes, and once you broke my nose with your head. You bumped it—hard. We cried together that time!" Her mother laughed.

Cora didn't see what was so funny. It sounded awful. *She* sounded awful.

"You were beautiful," said her mother, disengaging one arm from Evelyn and giving Cora's shoulder a squeeze. "You stopped traffic."

"So do fires," said Cora, smiling a little. "Remember that time you lost me at the zoo? You always said *I* wandered away. Maybe there's more to that story. Like you couldn't take all the crying anymore so you parked me by that wishing rock that looks like a frosted doughnut, told me to make a wish, and ran for the nearest exit."

"Very funny. That was one of the worst moments in my life, thinking I'd lost you," said her mother, and her eyes misted over at the memory. Cora felt gratified that her mother could still be so emotional about it after all these years. It was like when they were watching home movies once and her mother saw Charley hit Cora and try to push her off the seesaw. "Don't *do* that!" her mother had cried out, as if it was still happening right then and there, in the present.

"MAMA!" Evelyn was complaining again.

"Mom, how well do you know Mona?" Cora asked. Her mother was offering Evelyn a grape, and the baby was shaking her head furiously. "I'll have it," said Cora. "I like grapes."

"Look, Cora's having a grape," her mother said to the baby. "It's delicious, isn't it, Cora?"

"It's okay," said Cora.

Evelyn stared as the grape disappeared into

Cora's mouth. "Me!" she screamed. "MeMeMeMe!"

"Mom, how well do you know Mona?" Cora asked again.

"Not very well; why?" said her mother, still distracted by her failure to distract the baby.

Cora considered how to word what she was going to say next. She wasn't sure how much Evelyn could understand, and she didn't want to upset her even more. Suppose Mona doesn't come back? she thought. What would they tell Evelyn? What would they say when she grew up and asked what had happened on the beach the day her mother left her forever? Would they say that her mother loved her? But before Cora could speak, she spied Mona returning, running toward them with the milk.

"Lucky little Evelyn," she muttered, turning away. "Listen, I feel like taking a walk."

"Wait," said her mother. "We can go together." But Cora was already striding toward the ocean.

"Don't worry," she called over her shoulder, "I'll be back before the storm hits." And she broke into a run.

The surf was wild, churning white foam onto the shore. Cora jogged along, watching for sandpipers. She made a detour around a horseshoe crab, giving it a wide berth. Up ahead, a group of older kids were building a fire. They were having a hard time because of the wind. They gathered driftwood, then sat in a circle, as if performing some sort of religious rite. One girl in a bright green bikini cradled a bunch of corn in her arms and was feeding the half-peeled ears into the dying flame. Then she lay on her belly in the sand, moving her arms like wings. Two boys came up, lifted her, and swung her like a hammock, pretending to throw her into the sea. The boys were singing a sailor's heave-ho. And the girl was laughing so hard, she was almost choking.

Cora shivered, imagining some angered god rising from the smoke and showering them all with ash. She crept away and knelt some distance from them, in the doorway of one of the empty cabanas.

"Cora. Cora Eve!" She could hear her mother calling her.

A blurry figure appeared in her mind's eye, very tall, with features noble but indistinct. He was larger than life, superhuman, immortal. And he had loved her mother, Cora was sure. She forced her memory back, back before she was born. And for an instant, his shadow voice sounded and his shadow face took shape. But as he reached to embrace her, the voice turned to thunder. And the face dissolved into a shapeless smear of inky darkness on the distant horizon.

5
THE PO

Cora stood at the window, eating an apple, as great driving gusts of rain spattered the glass. She remembered the summer it had rained every day for two weeks and their street had become a river, rising and turning brown. Earthworms had crawled out of the park, spreading a stringy trail over the traffic islands on Broadway. When they died, they looked milky, like spaghetti left too long in the pot.

"Rain, rain, go away. Come again another day." Her mother was singing in the shower, preparing for an evening out. Cora frowned and began singing too, in a loud voice, "It rained and poured for forty days-ee days-ee. Rained and poured for forty days—ee days—ee. Drove those animals nearly crazy crazy. Children of the Lord," she bellowed. But her mother ignored her and continued with her nursery tune.

On the street just below, a runner passed by, getting wet. Suddenly, he doubled over and began massaging his calf. He wore bright orange socks that seemed to glow in the glare of the lamppost. His legs were muscular and slick. They looked detachable, like the plastic parts of a Cootie toy.

Cora thought of Charley. She had said she would play Cootie with him the other day, but then they had met the angel, and then they had quarreled so they had just never gotten around to it. Charley was supposed to come over tonight while her mother was out, but she hoped he had forgotten her promise, because she wasn't really in the mood for games.

Her mother slid into the room on a cloud of steam, still singing, but she stopped when she saw Cora's gloomy face. "What's up, Babe?" she asked. She stepped lightly into her special dressing alcove where perfume and powder and lipstick were all lined up in a row. Vigorously, she began toweling her hair dry, until it stood up in glossy points, like the studded manacles in a comic book chamber of torture. Even when she combed it flat, her hair was wavy, like Cora's, and could never be trusted to keep its shape.

"Are you seeing Roger?" Cora asked.

"Who else?" said her mother, sighing. "We're going dancing."

"But you don't even like him," Cora complained.

"Oh, I like him, Cora. He's a friend, after all. I never said I didn't like him. And he's a good dancer."

Cora couldn't imagine Roger doing anything but the polka. "Yeah, but you don't, you know, *like* him the way you liked my father, right?"

Her mother slipped a long gown over her head and spoke from under its layers. "That's right," she said, struggling to free her arms. "Could you come here and get the back for me, honey?"

The dress was riddled with hooks and snaps, and Cora patiently closed them one by one. She tried to imagine her mother getting ready to go dancing with her father, when they were first married. Was her mother just the same back then, singing in the shower and getting dressed, or could someone looking in tell the difference? Was it clear in those days that she was in love?

"Did you like being married?" Cora blurted out. "I mean . . ." She broke off. She wasn't sure what she meant.

Her mother smiled. "Do you remember Great-Aunt Sofie?" she asked.

"No. But did you hear my question?"

"She sang 'Yahka Hula Hickey Dula' on your birthday when you were four, and we visited her in

White Plains, don't you remember?"

"You're not listening," Cora said accusingly.

"You played Ping-Pong with her grandson in a basement full of owls."

"Owls?" Cora asked, giving up.

"Not live ones, darling—knickknacks, all sizes..."

"Why were they in her basement?"

"Because they were hideous."

"Did *she* think so?"

"Yes."

"Then why did she have so *many?*" Cora asked, intrigued in spite of herself.

"That's the point, sweetheart. Before she retired, a student of hers gave her a giant jug in the shape of an owl; she was too polite to throw it out. A friend saw it on her mantel and thought, 'Sofie likes owls!' so he brought her another, even larger. Sofie put it beside the first. People coming to call saw those big birds side by side above the fireplace and thought, 'Sofie likes owls.' Soon, there were dozens, all gifts. But poor Sofie never liked them."

"So?"

"So, Sofie never liked owls, but she found herself surrounded by them. And yes, I guess I liked being married, but I found myself alone. Life leads where it leads." Her mother sighed. "Who knows in advance where?"

"You *were* listening!" Cora said.

"I always listen," said her mother.

Cora rested her elbows on the dresser, staring at the framed photo of her mother and Roger on vacation in Bar Harbor. It had been taken shortly after they met, and she supposed they were more romantic then. They must have been, or her mother wouldn't have left her for four days to go off with him.

She remembered it well, staying at Charley's house, sitting around in his kitchen, a tiny space crowded by a sluggish washing machine which always seemed to be leaking soapy water onto the spotted linoleum floor, and a hulking refrigerator, usually empty except for orange juice and jars of jelly.

Mostly, they ate bananas and peanut butter sandwiches that week. Charley said his mother used to be a very good cook but she didn't have the heart for it anymore. She didn't seem to have the heart for much of anything, and Cora had felt kind of sorry for Charley.

Nothing worked in Charley's house, not even the lock on the front door. Someone had actually broken in and stolen their stereo but, despite her terror of being robbed again, Charley's mother had never replaced the lock. A wad of cotton plugged up the hole the burglar had left. Blocking the narrow hallway, though, was an intimidating collection of objects—bamboo poles poised to topple, piles of dusty books, a stack of unemptied handbags, rows of discarded shoes and sneakers, some of them stuffed with newspaper, and a fat jade green Buddha, precariously balanced on a heavy marble stand. "You're safe," she told Charley. "Only a true friend like me would risk her life to come in here."

"That's the general idea," he had answered. "Clever, isn't it?"

Depressing was more like it. Charley's TV didn't even work. Thick black vertical bands sandwiched all the elongated faces, pinching a bit more each night until, by the end of her stay, they had waned into darkness like the moon.

Her mother was powdering now, and Cora watched as she patted her nose and chin. She liked how her mother always did exactly the same thing in exactly the same order each time she used makeup. It made Cora feel safe.

Cora squinted at the snapshot again, really studying it for the first time. Instead of letting her mind wander back to what *she* had been doing while her mother was away, she tried to figure out what it had been like for her mother.

Of course, Roger looked ridiculous in his boxy bathing suit, posing in the bright sunshine with a child's pail on his head and waving a toy shovel at the camera. But her mother—why had Cora never noticed this before? Huddled against a dark cliff that plunged her into deep shadow, she seemed to be in a different picture. She was holding a baby bird in her palm. Framed by a kerchief tied tightly, her expression was sad, even saintly, like a painting Cora had once seen of Joan of Arc.

A moment later, Cora had been told, an attacking gull fell from the sky, defending its young, and Roger had grabbed her mother by the hand and fled. But the split-screen image showed them forever reigning in separate realms, comedy and tragedy. And a question seemed still to be hovering in her mother's solemn gaze, unanswered.

Cora threw herself down on the bed and propped her feet up on the pillow. Her eyes fell upon the book her mother had been reading at the beach, *The Town Beyond the Wall*, by Elie Wiesel. It was open.

"Is this the page you were going to read to me before?" she asked.

"Mmmmmmm?" asked her mother, blotting her darkened lips with a napkin, taking off half the color. Cora cleared her throat and recited:

"... 'You're afraid of me?'
'No.'
'But I'm Moishe the Madman. Aren't you afraid of crazy men?'
'No,' Michael said.
'That's good,' Moishe said. 'You should never be afraid of other people, even if they're crazy beyond the pale. The one man you have to be afraid of is yourself. But immediately the grave question arises: Who says that the others aren't you? Who says Moishe the Madman isn't you?'"

Cora read the passage to herself a second time. She raised her head, then sat up. "That's just what I said, isn't it?" she asked. "Who says we're not *all* crazy? You. Me. My father. The Mushroom. Miss Nancy. All of us. You're the one who's worried about Charley and me talking to crazies in the park. You're the one who says my father's crazy. This Moishe is nothing new to me."

Her mother turned from the mirror and gave Cora a long searching look. "Let's not fight tonight, honey," she said. "And let's not talk about your father, either, okay?" Her mother's tone clearly closed any further investigation into the past, at least for the evening.

Cora sighed. Her mind turned back to that horrible visit with Charley long ago. Charley had been beside himself looking forward to her coming, but when the time came, he hadn't exactly been the perfect host. Maybe he noticed that she was feeling sorry for him. Anyway, that week had almost ended their friendship.

In their shared room, he had constructed a flimsy barricade, which he patrolled with a water gun. In its shadow, he plotted campaigns to kidnap the few possessions Cora had brought with her with the aid of stinging ants, which he claimed lived in the sheets. For good measure, he had attached to the border between their two territories a clown bank with a tongue that took plastic tokens, and he demanded to be paid whenever she crossed to use the bathroom, which was on *his* side.

But the worst memory was the game he had invented one night: The Po—an invisible poison butterfly, bred in a laboratory at Columbia University and released into the park by mistake.

"And now," Charley had whispered in a hoarse voice, "it's *in this room.* . . ." Anyone it brushed with its wings would die instantly, he said. The only way to avoid that sorry fate was to stay at strict attention, quiet as a tree trunk, until it finished circling. It wouldn't land on anything standing still.

"It's only a game," Charley had laughed afterward, breaking the spell, but Cora had been rigid for at least a half hour after that. And whenever Charley invoked the Po, which he did a few more times, she would go into the same rigor mortis against her will, half believing that each choked breath would be her last.

She hadn't thought of the Po for ages. Even now, it still gave her the shivers. Yet silently, she forgave Charley once again. She always forgave Charley. If they were to fight and not make up, who would keep her up to date on animals in the zoos of the world? Who would explain the wobble of the earth upon its axis, the evaporation of rain, the grinding of glaciers from the Pleistocene to the present? Who would point out that the sky and sea don't truly meet at the horizon, and that her heart was the size of a clenched fist?

6
THE LAMP

"There was a mad man
And he had a mad wife
And they lived in a mad town
Till they had a daughter
Oh, she was mad too
And she turned them upside down."

Cora's breath was coming short as she jumped faster and faster through the house, practicing. Her mother didn't like her to jump rope indoors. But her mother had left on her date with Roger, and Cora loved the feeling of doing something very noisy and large in their small apartment. Her feet made satisfying pounding noises on the wooden floorboards as she hopped from room to room. Sometimes, her rope hit the walls with a sharp crack.

48

"The father was mad
The mother was mad
And the girl was mad beside.
Upon a mad bull they all of them got
And madly away did ride."

She was gasping now and would have to stop. She threw her rope aside and fell into a chair. Above the sound of her own panting, she could hear the wheels of Charley's mother's shopping cart bumping up the steps. Charley had said he would borrow it and bring over the birthday present he had for her.

Cora wasn't angry at him anymore, but she wondered if *he* was still angry. Usually he was the one who stayed angry the longest. She heard a shuffling and a cough and then a loud knock on the front door. Cora looked through the spy hole. Charley was staring into it. As soon as her eye met his, he started singing at the top of his lungs: "Oh it's Monday, la la, then Tuesday, la la, then Wednesday, la la, then Thursday, la la, then Friday, la la, then Saturday, la la, then Sunday—that makes the week."

He wore a twisted towel on his head like a turban, half crushed as if it had been caught under the wheels of a bus. Cora opened the door and he just blinked, not budging an inch. One hand rested on a billowing brown garbage bag in which, she supposed, he had wrapped her present.

"Hi," he said. "I'm Snefru, Monarch of Magic." He looked more like a scarecrow tricked into jumping off its pole. "Do muffin crumbs sabotage your one-slot toaster?" he asked, holding up a finger. "Does mold attack the dwarfed fronds of your Florida mail-order palm tree? Do leaves of falling plaster mix with the soy juices of your stir-fried supper? When you take salmon skin out of the can, does the gray skin mash in with the meat? Do your windows stick? If you answer 'yes' to any or all of these questions, then you need Snefru. May I come in?"

Cora knew he was overacting to cover up their quarrel. She stepped aside, and he saluted and marched past her, maneuvering his burden on creaking wheels. "All yours, Madame," he said when he had parked it in the middle of her mother's bedroom. "I am at your service." And he bowed.

"Snefru can turn your bread into beer, your eggs into chickens. Snefru can pull thirty fleas from your nose. Snefru can spin you on your head like a top. He can take your teeth and return them whiter than they were. He can make a penny jump into your hat. He can swallow himself. And he can sneeze loudly." And he sneezed.

Then he pulled a chair over to the mystery package and sat down, as if to guard it. Cora laughed and began tearing away at the plastic, but before she could even guess at what it was, Charley held up both hands. "Wait," he said. "I better prepare you for this. I mean, this object is familiar to you. But what you don't know is how to *use* it."

He paused and took a deep breath. "There's a secret here, you see. That is . . ." He broke off and Cora realized he was no longer kidding or putting on a show. Snefru was gone, and Charley had become serious. She stood close to him and waited.

"You have dreams about finding your dad," he said softly, studying the floor. "I used to have dreams about my dad being dead. Which he *is*, but the dreams were weird.

"I mean, for example . . ." He took another breath. "Sometimes, he and I were walking through the inside of a turtle—one of those giant ones on a tropical island? We were holding hands and just walking, you know, like we were in the woods, only we weren't seeing trees and rocks—we were passing the turtle heart and the turtle lungs and liver, and the turtle kidneys and intestines till we came out the other end. When I looked around, my dad wasn't with me though. He was still *inside*, and the turtle just got up and slid into the ocean."

Charley tipped back in his chair until he wobbled in space, smiling tightly. "Nice, hunh?"

Cora shook her head. "Not so nice, no," she whispered.

Charley's chair came forward with a bang, and he gazed at her. "Okay, well, I know all that isn't very 'happy birthday,' is it? But I was trying to think of what you really *needed* for your birthday. I was thinking about you looking for your dad, and then I was remembering about those dreams I used to have, and that's when it came to me.

"See, when the nightmares woke me up, I'd go into our living room and I'd turn on this lamp I'm going to give you, and I'd stare into it. For about an hour, I'd just look at it, and after a while, I started talking to it. I was really talking to my dad, telling him about everything that was happening. And, this sounds crazy, I know, but he answered! That is, the lamp answered, but it was his voice. It didn't work with any other lamp either, just this one." He paused. "Okay," he said, "now you can open it."

But before Cora could make a move, Charley ripped the rest of the covering off and held up the lamp as if it were an animal trying to escape. It was large and heavy and quite dusty. Cora recognized it from Charley's house, but she studied it more carefully now that she knew its history.

A painting of green cacti the same round shape as the base itself gave it a Mexican look. In the painted shadow of the tallest cactus, a fat man was in the act of sneaking a siesta, his sombrero completely covering his face. Charley looked embarrassed now that the present and its purpose had been revealed.

"It works best when you're alone," he said, "like in the middle of the night, when your mom's asleep."

"My mom never sleeps, even in the middle of the night," said Cora. "Whenever I wake up from a bad dream or something, she's always awake too." Cora hesitated. She considered telling Charley about the time she had found her mother making the scrapbook but decided against it. He had told her a secret, but it was his to tell. The other was kind of her mother's secret.

"Let's try the lamp right now," she said. "*We're* alone."

Charley shook his head, his face clouding. "I don't want to be here when you do it," he said.

Cora wondered if Charley still needed the lamp.

"Don't you ever have dreams about your dad anymore?" she asked, rising.

"No," he said, looking away. "Hey, I brought you a book, too—about angels. You're not still mad about the notebook, are you?"

"I called you, didn't I?" she said, opening the book. "*They look upon the mercy seat,*" she read. "*The universe is their library. They see all things, past, present, and future. They separate sheep from goats. They blow trumpets and their feet are like polished brass.*"

She closed the book. This was fine as a peace offering, but it didn't look too promising. "Thanks," she said, placing it carefully on her mother's night table. "I'll read it later."

"You're welcome," said Charley, grinning. "So what's for dinner? How about a nice platter of newt eyes, some sea cucumbers braised in brown sauce, dog kabob, and a great big carafe of penguin dust?"

"Didn't you eat before you came over?" asked Cora, laughing.

"Snefru is always hungry," he answered, rubbing his hands together.

"Never mind Snefru. You sound just like the Mushroom."

"I *am* the Mushroom in disguise," he said. "You know, I think I figured out his suitcase? I read a story about this guy who goes to parties. He never talks to anyone, just hangs around the edges, listening and noticing everyone's moves. You know, like how they pat their hair, how they hitch up their stockings, how they spit into their hankies, how they check for food between their teeth? And he tapes it all and makes it into this very high, strange music, and then carries the tape around in a black suitcase. Get it? It's perfect."

Cora didn't answer. She wasn't interested in the Mushroom or his suitcase. She was thinking about the angel. She wondered if he was still in his spot on the library steps or if he had gone elsewhere, bringing some other kid a message.

"Listen, Cora, were you jumping when I rang the bell? I thought I heard you jumping," said Charley. "I'm kind of your coach, so I have to tell you, I'm worried."

"Well, I'm not. I just don't care about the tournament this year."

"Maybe *you* don't, but Zeffy does. I've seen her in the playground and she's good."

"Well, maybe the judges'll give awards for the rhymes this time. I've been finding some nice ones," said Cora. "It could be like the Miss America talent show. I could just stand still like this and recite." She drew herself up to her full height.

"Flying man, flying man
  Up in the sky,
  Where are you going to
  Flying so high?

"Over the city
  And over the sea,
  Flying man, flying man,
  Can't you take me?"

"Hey, I like it," said Charley. But I don't think it's going to get you very far with the judges. "Maybe you could develop a *new* talent."

"Yeah, like making pots. I've been liking my ceramics club a lot lately. How about I just bring my pots?"

"No, too dull," said Charley. "I mean something daring like the hula. I heard of a Miss America contestant who wowed the jury by doing the hula. The only thing was she got carried away. Even after she won, she danced around all day in her tea-leaf skirt, beating on gourds with bamboo sticks. She even let her hair grow to the ground and kept her old fingernails in a box by her bed."

"What?"

"Yeah, hula dancers aren't supposed to cut their hair or their fingernails. So she cut her nails but then she saved them. I didn't make it up, honestly.

I read about it in the newspaper."

He began to hula around the room, swiveling his hips convincingly. "Oooeeelayeeeooo," he crowed. Cora joined in, swaying and orbiting Charley. They held hands and leaned back, spinning around faster and faster. Then laughing, they collapsed on the floor, near her mother's makeup table. They lay there, staring at the ceiling until their laughter slowly died, and then awhile longer, breathing loudly.

Through half-closed eyes Cora took in her eye-level surroundings. Everything looked oddly bright and beautiful. Scarves spilled out of a drawer, and a tangle of necklaces hung on the knob. Cora stared at the beads, drinking in shapes and colors as if she'd never seen her mother's jewelry or any jewelry before. A pile of discarded panty hose in the corner caught her attention, then a dish filled with pennies, then an open basket of buttons. In that familiar space, nothing looked familiar.

I guess I've never seen it quite from this angle before, she thought, and just as the thought registered, her eye fell upon a box wedged under the bottom drawer. It was covered with dust. She sat up straight and pulled it toward her, forcing it from its hiding place and, in the process, crushing it a bit. Charley sat up too.

"Charley," she whispered. Slowly, she lifted the lid, revealing a thick stack of letters on crackly thin blue paper. Aerogrammes. Addressed to Greece. All in her mother's handwriting.

7
THE LETTERS

Cora drew one of the letters out, reading silently.

Dear Nikos,

It's Halloween and I haven't heard from you in almost a month. Your last letter sounded so distant. And now, nothing. I feel I've done something wrong. Maybe it's a simple thing that can be corrected simply, if you'd just tell me.

It's Halloween, as I said, and I'm sitting here thinking about witches. Did you know they were executed by the score in Salem? I'm reading about some poor woman who made an apple dumpling. The court said she couldn't have gotten the apple inside the dumpling without the devil's help. She proved she wasn't a witch by making a dumpling in court. Can I prove my innocence to you just as simply?

Nikos, it's so hard when you're not here to talk to, face

to face. But then, it was hard when you were here too. Please write!

All my love,

Sara

Cora sat with the letter in her lap. It didn't sound like her mother at all. She met Charley's inquiring stare, hesitated, then passed him the letter without a word and took up the next.

Dear Nikos,

I think the baby is a girl. If I'm right, I want to name her Cora. Cora Eve.

I've been remembering my own girlhood these days. I used to be very good at jump rope, did I ever tell you that? But for some reason I stopped jumping when I was about eleven or twelve and became a steadyender. Do you know what that is? It means I never got to jump. I just turned the rope for the other kids.

Why I agreed to it, I no longer remember. All I know is that something that once made me happy turned into torture. One minute, I was champion, doing high arcs in the air like a kangaroo. And the next, I was out of the action, watching the others do what I could do better, without a prayer of joining in.

I could have played the steadyender for just one day

and then come back—more powerful than ever—leaping higher and faster than anyone. Instead, I waited for my friends to release me. And they never did.

So, I just stopped playing. And the importance of the game faded, except that I've always been ashamed of having accepted reduced circumstances without a fight.

Nikos, I know I'm losing you. But how can I fight when you won't answer? I feel like the steadyender again, turning, turning, turning while the rope grows heavier and memories of better days grow dim.

And again, I'm waiting for the release.

All my love,
Sara

When Cora raised her head, Charley was looking at her, waiting.

"My mother was good at jump rope," she said lamely. "Like me. It says so here." She couldn't meet his eyes. "Listen, Charley, maybe you should go home now."

"But I'm supposed to stay here with you and sleep over. My mother's out too and anyway, it's late."

Cora looked at Charley's stricken face and sighed. "Oh well, I guess you can stay," she said.

"Why don't I go cook us some frankfurters—and

popcorn?" he suggested, rising.

She nodded. "Sounds great," she said. "I'll just sit here awhile longer and then we can eat, okay?"

Charley dropped the first letter on the floor and beat a hasty retreat to the kitchen, closing the door behind him. She listened to his steps going down the hall. Why were all the letters from her mother? she wondered. Hadn't they been mailed? She checked the stamps. Yes, they were canceled. Hadn't her father ever answered them?

Suddenly, she felt uncomfortable sitting in her mother's room. It was as if her mother were there, reading over her shoulder. She gathered up the letters, stuffed them back into the box, and carried them into her own room. She settled down to read again but something was still wrong. She got up and went back, looking around distractedly. Ah yes, the lamp. She picked it up and lugged it down the hall, placing it carefully on the floor beside her. Again, she began to read.

Dearest Nikos,

I feel that you left me long before this, and were only being honest by placing so great a distance between us. At least now, we write to one another. Or anyway, I write to you.

You couldn't have known things would take this turn,

of course, but I can't help blaming you. Would you have
stayed with me, had you known?

   I no longer walk down the street feeling tipped off
balance because your arm isn't around me. Instead, I live
day to day, waiting for our daughter to be born. Me—a
mother. It's so hard to take in. And you—a father. Or
maybe not. Nikos, that's up to you. I do miss you. But
Cora doesn't need half a father—a man who comes and
goes and hurts her each time he goes.

   Come and stay, or don't come at all.

Love still and always,

Sara

Cora riffled through the next few aerogrammes. All the handwriting was her mother's. Her father *must* have written back after that last one. A terrible thought entered her mind. Had her mother destroyed his answers along with the photos? Please, let it not be true, she prayed. She came across a longer letter, folded into an envelope and opened it eagerly.

Dear Nikos,

   Do you think it's all because we didn't have a large
enough wedding? I've just been reading a book of sewing
instructions: "Begin by tying a small knot so it won't
show but not so small that it pulls out." Ours is pulling

out, isn't it? Or at least, you're pulling out.

You say your mind is made up. I have to get that through my head. I just can't believe it, that's all. I'd have an easier time believing it if it were only me you weren't returning to. But Cora Eve! The night she was born, I stayed up all night, just staring at her—watching her breathe. She's that beautiful!

Cora closed her eyes. So he had answered. He had said he didn't want to be a father—her father. She sat perfectly still, then opened her eyes again.

The afternoon you took off for Greece, you left half a carved-out cantaloupe on the windowsill. It changed shape and collected rainwater. I kept it for over a week and I cried when I finally threw it away.

Now I can't bear to have your things around, reminding me of you.

Cora began to tremble. Here it comes, she thought. Now, here it comes.

Today, I threw out all your avocado plants. I lined them up in the hallway with a sign on each: SAVE ME. Maybe some neighbor will take pity on them.

I also did away with that plastic bread box you bought—the one that clacked shut like bad dentures. And the suitcase you left behind that looked like a giant lunch bag. And your packing crate slats and chips of stained

glass you were saving for future constructions. And your
bag of souvenir matchbooks. All your junk, in short.
Except for your ties, which I sometimes wear myself. And
your birdcage.

I'm sitting here now, eating an entire pumpkin pie,
drinking brandy, and listening to "Bad Dream Blues" as
the ceiling falls down in little flakes because of the damp
or the heat or maybe the music.

I'd like all my letters back, please. I don't know if I'm
going to burn them or keep them for when Cora is old
enough to understand. But I'm going to burn all of
yours, I know that much. And all my photographs of you.
And all my photographs of the two of us. I just haven't
worked up to it yet.

There's an old Russian saying: Hair by hair you can
pluck out the whole beard. I intend to pluck you out.

Cora ran her fingers over the last line, blindly
tracing the words. She felt sick. Carefully, she took
all the blue aerogrammes out of the box and
spread them on the floor. Then, stripping off her
socks and shoes, she walked over them, treading
heavily from one to the other. The dry leaves
didn't crackle as she expected. They didn't tear
either but remained flat and utterly silent.

In the eerie stillness, she trudged around and

around in circles, bearing down as hard as she could. Finally, she threw herself down on top of them, and began to sob so deeply that she never noticed Charley, who opened the door and watched for a while before slipping silently away.

8
BAUBO

Still sobbing, Cora fell asleep. She dreamed she had returned to the little Greek village and to Baubo, her guide. Baubo was leading her along some railroad tracks in the moonlight toward a cemetery set in a grove of cedar trees. "I'll show you my father's grave," she said, taking Cora's hand.

They wandered down an aisle of what looked to Cora like rabbit hutches. In each stood a tall black urn of ashes and a framed photograph of a father, mother, or child—or of a family, all together. It was like the Silverpoint cabanas, only these people were dead. A chill lodged itself between Cora's shoulder blades, and she heard a strange hum in the air.

Baubo stopped by a tabernacle, larger than the others, which they entered on their hands and knees, crawling. The hum grew louder. Inside, the walls were painted with angels. The angels were armored in tin suits but their wings and heads were exposed. Their large eyes were trained upon the ceiling, which was sprinkled with stars, like the ones Cora got on spelling tests.

Crouching, Cora studied the angels and considered praying. She had never really prayed before, but this seemed a very good time to start.

"Please," she whispered to the nearest angel. "Help me." And the painted angel answered, "*Pos apo tho?*" She remembered that phrase from her *Teach Yourself Greek* book. *What brings you here?*

She looked around for Baubo to translate her answer, but the girl had disappeared. She was all alone.

"Eenie meanie jelly beanie, the spirits are about to speak," she whispered, edging out of the little church backward. The hum grew louder. She remembered reading somewhere that children who talked to themselves were always very bright. The article mentioned some genius in Hawaii who had five imaginary husbands in the first grade. They rode by her side on the school bus, and she scolded them loudly for throwing salt at cars. Salt. Cora tasted it on her tongue. And the hum grew louder still.

Cora whirled around. Coming straight toward her was a giant dressed in purple running shorts, holding an enormous watermelon in his arms. Strapped to his thigh was a thick black belt from which a long shiny knife dangled. Humming to himself, he strode powerfully down the lane.

Cora wanted to run the other way. But she was lost. "*Hameni*," she blurted. "*Ime hameni.* I'm lost."

The veins in the giant's neck stood out like roads on a relief map as he hoisted the heavy watermelon higher. "*Alati*," he mumbled, and winked. Salt. Then he jabbed his huge finger toward the bleached plain that stretched before them in the moonlight.

Cora left the path she had been following and hurried forward. But the salt immediately flaked away, and it was hard to walk.

"Maybe I'm dead," Cora thought, "and I'm taking a walk on dried tears."

The salt plain led to a marina, where schooners floated near a rickety wooden pier in water so calm it looked solid. Cora headed toward the dock, which was dotted with shacks. They were empty and tilted, as if lifted by some terrible turbulence under the sea. Cora thought she heard the high unsteady notes of a violin in the distance. The tune was cheering.

She sat down on the warm planks, as the music came closer, faded, then came closer again. Soon, a chain of dancers snaked past, arms linked.

The men rapped out lightning patterns with their feet. Moving more slowly, the women swayed, the fringes of their shawls hanging down like silkworms. They circled Cora, shouting and waving. Then, hoisting her from her seat, they pinned her to the tail of their procession.

They neared a village square where two baby lambs roasting on a spit sent up a wavering column of smoke and showered ashes on an infant in ruffles who poked at the fire with a forked stick. A piglet ran loose through the crowd. Strung with pinpoint lights, a flowering tree lit up the dancers, who were now weaving Cora into their ranks.

A girl broke from the dance and elbowed toward Cora, cradling a bunch of candy eggs in her palm. "Baubo!" Cora called, relieved to see her again. "Where *were* you?"

Baubo sneezed, not answering, then took Cora's hand and pressed the treats into it. She pulled Cora out of the dance toward a watering trough, where a few other children were wading and splashing.

"Have you found my father?" Cora asked her urgently. But again, Baubo didn't answer. She stooped and slapped Cora's shoes, making signs for her to take them off and play in the water. Cora drew back.

Baubo broke away then and ran to a dark man in uniform, who was standing on the sidelines, staring through heavy binoculars at the heavens. He wore a big-brimmed paper hat and Cora couldn't see his face. After what seemed like a heated argument between them, he let himself be led over to Cora and strung the binoculars around her neck, nodding magnanimously and pointing upward.

Overcome with a certain sense of disaster, Cora looked through the glass at the amber moon. Descending, it slid under her ribs, pumping honey into her bones. Rims of the craters stood out razor sharp. The sky seemed to have fallen onto her shoulders like Chicken Licken's sky.

Trembling, she lowered the lenses. Her eyes swam as firm hands gripped her waist. *Nikos?* It came out a whimper.

Her father waltzed her around the other children very sedately, while spray from their game wet her dress and, mingling with her tears of joy, settled on her rumpled hair, a cold crown of mist.

But she still could not see his face.

9
THE BUTTERFLY

The first thing Cora saw when she woke was Charley's lamp. It seemed to be glowing, though she had never turned it on. She stared at it. Where was Charley? He must have seen her crying and left.

She checked each room, calling his name softly. Yes, he had gone home. She returned to the lamp and rested her cheek against the base. It felt cool and comforting. "Baubo," she whispered. "Baubo, listen. Come to me here." She ran her hand over the porcelain. It had seemed perfectly smooth a moment before, but she noticed some scars now, as if a secret scattershot message in code had settled into the surface.

"Answer me, if you hear me," she pleaded. "Baubo!" But the lamp didn't answer. It wasn't going to work for her.

"You're a dim old thing," she mumbled, rocking back on her heels. Her mother's letters were spread out over the floor and the box, slightly crushed, looked too small to hold them all. She began putting them back, then stopped.

There was one she hadn't seen before, stuck inside the lid and almost hidden by the cardboard flaps, which were coming undone. It wasn't in her mother's handwriting. In fact, it looked more like a drawing, but it was signed, *Love, Nikos*. And it wasn't addressed to her mother either but to her. *Dear Cora*, it said. Was she dreaming? She looked more closely.

It was a beautiful picture, elaborately drawn and colored, of a butterfly and a mazelike map of its itinerary—a tortuous route leading to an open flower. Labels indicated that Cora was the flower and her father was the butterfly. But there were so many detours between one and the other that their reunion looked as if it would take place in the very distant future if such a labyrinthian path could be followed at all. And the intricate diagram had no words other than *Dear Cora . . . Love, Nikos*.

Cora took a deep breath. It seemed to her that the Po had made a comeback. The poison butterfly had landed on her at last, and her heart had grown too large for her chest.

How many times had she asked her mother if her father had ever written to her? Her mother had lied. The phrase "old enough to understand" floated back to her from the letters. She wondered bitterly when her mother would have considered her old enough to understand.

"Cora doesn't need half a father—a man who comes and goes. . . ." her mother had written. But most of the kids at school had one parent or another coming and going, living somewhere else. Everyone was divorced. A part-time dad was better than none. What gave her mother the right to decide for her?

Cora clenched her fists and gazed angrily at Charley's lamp again. She felt hot all over. It had been a mistake to try to talk to Baubo through the lamp when it was her father she wanted to reach. The lamp was probably only for missing fathers—hers and Charley's. She knelt beside it again as the thin soprano voice of a much younger child rose in her throat, warbling dismally.

> *"Father, oh father, oh where are you roving?*
> *Over the sea, over the sea.*
> *Father, oh father, oh who are you loving?*
> *All that love me, that love me."*

It was a song she had learned in school a long time ago, but she wasn't certain she had the words right. It didn't matter, though. Her father would hear her now and understand how much she needed him. Together they would fly far away over the dark sea, away from her mother, mounting higher and higher until the volcanic heat in her veins burst into a pure, undying flame.

"Father, oh father, oh where are you roving?
Over the dell, over the dell.
Father, oh father, oh who are you loving?
All that sleep well, that sleep well."

Cora thought she heard her mother's key in the door. She swept the pile of letters under her bed along with the box. But she held on to the butterfly note as she leaped beneath her blanket. Hiding the evidence under her body, she imitated a corpse, folding her hands over her chest. Then she scissored into an upright position, and checked the room. Yes, it looked normal except for the lamp. She took her sleeping pose again. "Don't come too close," she prayed silently. "And don't kiss me."

Her mother tiptoed in and hovered, fumbling with her handbag. Lightly, she touched Cora's forehead. Cora wanted to slap her hand away but she continued to play dead. "Honey, are you awake? Charley's not here. Cora?"

Her mother sighed and went into the living room. Cora heard her dialing and talking to

Charley's mom. She couldn't make out the words, but it sounded as if Charley was asleep too, or pretending to be.

Cora didn't think she would ever sleep again. She listened for all the familiar night sounds. Her mother brushing her teeth and shuffling around in her slippers. The car horns. The trees rustling in the park.

A gang of construction workers congregated noisily below her window. She looked out at them. Their yellow helmets gleamed like knobs on a control panel, half hiding their moonlike faces, which seemed suspended over the street. They gestured robotically, dressed in boots and slickers the size of tents although it was no longer raining. Like medieval doctors applying leeches to a fevered city, they heaved a manhole cover onto their shoulders, releasing a solid column of white hot steam that escaped with a violent and continuous hiss.

10

HOT POTATO

Cora wanted to lie down and rest, but she was riveted to her sentry post, watching the sunrise. She hadn't slept all night. Charley had once told her how, at Bedouin weddings, roast camel was served but inside the camel the guests would find sheep and inside the sheep there would be chickens and inside the chickens there would be fish and so on. Standing by her window, staring into the changing light, Cora felt as if she had just swallowed all those things.

Yawning, she rolled her heavy head from side to side and stretched. Her neck ached and she could no longer trust her eyes. A moment before she thought she had seen a big bear passing by but realized, as the animal came closer, that it was just a woman in a brown sweater. And the treetops across the way had seemed, a while ago, to suddenly melt into one mighty green wave, moving in the morning wind, stirring her with wonder. But it had lasted only an instant and then they had looked like everyday trees again.

So when she saw Miss Nancy trundling toward her, she shook her head, trying to shake the vision away. Maybe it was some other bag lady, or maybe it was no bag lady at all, just an early riser, disheveled from her walk.

The woman was truly homely, dressed in battered boots shaped as if there were more than the usual toes crammed inside and rolled down to mid-calf, revealing thick scabs like dragon scales. Her legs were red and swollen, and she looked dirty except for her blouse, which was white with a starched collar and a repeating pattern of birds.

She walked slowly down the block, cradling a carton of eggs in her hands. And then she did something remarkable. She began cracking the eggs on the hoods of standing cars and depositing the yolks one by one all in a row so that they trembled like gold in the soft glow of dawn.

Cora's mouth dropped open. It *was* Miss Nancy; she was sure of it now. Wait until she told Charley.

Miss Nancy crossed the street to the park and settled on a bench. Opening a large black plastic bag, she drew out a loaf of bread and began tearing at it, tossing the pieces onto the cobblestones.

"One to rot, one to grow, one for the pigeon, one for the crow," she called out loudly. And the pigeons gathered. Cora could no longer hear what Miss Nancy was saying, but she looked content in the early morning light, conversing with the birds.

Cora turned away and tiptoed to her bureau, opening the top drawer very quietly. She drew out her jewelry box and the small red velvet pouch where she kept her father's signature. Unfolding the slightly ragged piece of paper, she read it again. *Nikos Pavlides.*

She brought it over to her bed where she had left the butterfly letter. Yes, it was the same *Nikos*, spiky and a little cramped. Cora placed them both carefully dead center on her quilt, so that her mother couldn't miss them should she wake before Cora returned.

Slipping on her socks, she held her shoes in one hand and crept down the hall. She heard no sounds coming from her mother's room. Maybe she's asleep, for once, she thought.

Long ago, Charley had suggested sneaking out "at cock's crow" and meeting in the park, but Cora had been too frightened. Now she didn't feel scared at all as she shut the front door slowly without a creak, locked it, and hurried down the stairs.

For an instant, she wondered what her mother

would think. Maybe she should have left her a note. But then, what would the note have said? If her mother worried, it was her own fault. She deserved to worry. Let her think Cora had run away.

The air was colder than she expected but it felt good on her face. And there was a fresh, flowery scent that sometimes lingered after a rain.

Miss Nancy seemed to recognize Cora as soon as she approached. Up close, she had one green eye and one blue eye, and both were steely like holes in a street grate. Her hair was stiff with a jagged part down the middle, like the edge of a Popsicle split in two.

"The early bird gets the bread," she said, pointing to the flock that had congregated around her, pecking greedily. "Remember that." Behind her in the grass, three squirrels stood on their hind legs and nodded in unison, their tails waving.

Miss Nancy popped an entire slice of bread into her mouth and chewed with exaggerated gusto. Then, brushing the crumbs from her skirt, she handed Cora a battered piece of cardboard. Scrawled in capital letters across the top were the words from a song Cora used to like to sing: "There was an old lady who swallowed a horse. She's dead, of course." And neatly pasted below was a news item: DISAPPOINTED WITH HER HUSBAND,

WHO HAD REFUSED TO TAKE HER TO NIAGARA FALLS
FOR THEIR ANNIVERSARY, A SHOPKEEPER SWALLOWED
TWENTY-ONE NAILS, SIX WINDOW BOLTS, ONE HUN-
DRED AND TWO PINS, A STONE, AND THREE PIECES OF
GLASS.

"That's awful," said Cora, passing the story back
to Miss Nancy.

"Not so awful as most," said Miss Nancy.

Cora thought of her mother in the middle of the
night, cutting clippings out of the newspaper. Who
was crazy after all? The angel and Miss Nancy? Or
her father who walked on hot coals? Or Charley
who talked to a lamp? Or her mother who couldn't
sleep and who told lies?

Cora shivered, and the nearest pigeon, startled,
flew up into her face. "Miss Nancy, why do you like
pigeons so much?" she asked, shooing it away.
Then she added, "My friend Charley wants to
know."

Miss Nancy picked at a loose thread on her
sleeve. "Let him ask me himself then," she said. "I
answer questions on Mondays." She offered Cora
another card, much harder to decipher than the
first. Cora squinted at it, trying to make sense out
of the blotchy handwriting.

"Food and beverages cause cancer," it said.
"Shells of the crab and scales of the fish cause

paralysis and stroke. Horns of the bull cause Horn & Hardart. I live in the Hotel Riverside. Lady Moon. Room Twenty-two."

"Lady Moon?" Cora asked.

Suddenly, she remembered the real words of that song she had been singing the night before. There was no "father, oh father" in it at all. It went:

> *Lady Moon, Lady Moon, where are you roving?*
> *Over the sea, over the sea.*
> *Lady Moon, Lady Moon, who are you loving?*
> *All that love me, that love me.*

Miss Nancy studied Cora through her green eye, closing the blue. "That's what they call me," she said. "I'm not saying I'm the best clairvoyant ever was or ever will be. But I was born with three veils on my head. Three, folded one inside the other," she repeated, holding up three fingers.

"Do you really see into the future?" Cora asked.

Miss Nancy put her palms to her forehead and pressed, as if she had a headache. Then she sucked in a deep breath and, puffing out her cheeks, let it out slowly. "Mondays," she said, dismissing Cora. "You bring your friend."

Cora said good-bye and walked quickly away down the path. She hoped Charley would want to visit Lady Moon. She needed to know, now more than ever, when her father would be arriving, but she didn't dare go alone.

The sky was lighter now, and more people had come out into the park. She moved toward the playground, vaguely hoping she could join in a game of jump rope, but she knew it was probably still too early for that. The sun had burned through the clouds and felt warm on the top of her head. She put one foot directly in front of the other as if balancing on a high wire, admiring her red shoes against the dark asphalt.

Just ahead, a young couple sauntered along, pushing a stroller. They moved so slowly, she was catching up to them. Suddenly their toddler let out a howl and raised his arms, indicating he wanted to be carried. "Mommy, *up!*" he cried.

The mother lifted him, smiling, and the child hugged her close. Then he stretched out his arms to his father. "Daddy!" he cried, and he was passed from one parent to the other.

"Hot potato!" the woman sang out, and ran ahead. The man began to run too, and the boy bounced up and down in his arms, letting out deep growls of laughter as he was handed over to his mother again.

"Hot potato!" shouted his father, and they continued the game, passing their small son back and forth over and over again.

Cora stood at attention, watching the scene. Mother Child. Father Child. Father Mother Child. If that kid lost his father, she thought, the memory of the hot potato game would still be inscribed somewhere in his brain—the two big happy faces, like the north and south poles, one on either side of his own.

The little boy rolled his head back, gazing rapturously at the clouds from the safe height of his father's shoulders. And the realization struck Cora harder than it ever had before, taking her breath away: She would *never* know how it felt to grow up with two parents who loved her. If her father returned tomorrow, she would still never know.

11

THE STEADYENDER

There was only one other kid in the playground when Cora entered, a spindly boy sitting on a bench just inside the black gate. He was hunched over, playing half-heartedly with a plastic phonograph he had wedged between his knees, changing the records over and over again until finally he settled on a chirping tune about a hedgehog. It was a toy designed for a much younger child. He looked up sadly at Cora as her shadow touched his shoe. Abruptly, the song stopped.

Cora halted involuntarily, wondering why he was looking at her so intently. Was it because they were the only people there so early, or did he know her? Slowly, he put his music box aside and removed a paper bag from his pocket. On one bare knee, he unwrapped a chocolate cupcake and then took a bite, his eyes glinting behind his glasses as he swallowed.

"Hi," he said, as if just remembering how to speak. "Want some?" He held up the rest of the cupcake, his skinny arm blocking her retreat, the waxy edges of the bakery paper pushing toward her like the ruffles on a new tooth.

"No thanks," she said. He looked pitiful, sitting there, eating all by himself. He shrugged and continued to eat. Between mouthfuls, he said, "My name's Calvin—what's yours?"

"Cora," she said.

"Nice to meet you. Why don't you sit down?" he asked, brightening.

"Listen, Calvin, I'd like to but I'm looking for some friends." She stopped. That didn't sound right. This kid looked as if he had no friends at all. And she didn't either, really, except for Charley. Why was she talking that way?

"Oh," he said, bowing his head.

"See, I need to jump rope because . . . there's this contest and I haven't been jumping . . . and if I don't start soon, I may as well give it up. . . ." She couldn't believe she was standing there, trying to explain about the tournament to this weird boy, but he made her feel bad, looking so alone.

He didn't answer but offered her his treat again, thrusting it upon her. She stepped back, but not before some of the icing smeared on her skirt.

"There's a game starting over there, I think," he said, pointing.

She looked across the large cement arena where she usually practiced. It was deserted, the rusted sprinkler rising stumplike from the center. But he was right. Now she noticed a group of girls all the way over by the south gate. They were milling around, getting ready to start, and she thought she spotted Zeffy among them.

"Thanks, Calvin," she said, moving off.

"Good-bye," he said, and gave her a big grin. She smiled back, relieved. He looked like a regular little kid when he smiled.

"See you around."

"Yeah."

Feeling a little less lonely than before, Cora strode toward the girl who looked like Zeffy. She glanced back over her shoulder to wave good-bye to Calvin, but he had aleady gone back to his cupcake, chewing steadily.

Cora sighed. Yes, it *was* Zeffy, in the center of things, organizing the others. Her face was kind of pale and puffy, her eyes heavily lidded like a lizard's. Now that she was no longer fat, her head always looked very long to Cora, reminding her of pictures she had seen in school of those stone heads on Easter Island, leftovers from some vanished tribe people could only guess about.

Zeffy already had her lineup, but she waved to Cora and indicated a place for her at the head of the line, right after Zeffy herself.

Cora put her hands in her pockets and shuffled over, slouching. "Hi," she said, but her voice came out a croak.

"I haven't seen you here in a long time," said Zeffy, squinting against the sun. "Wanna jump?"

"Yeah, I guess so, thanks," said Cora.

Zeffy nodded and turned to her friends. "Okay," she said, and the ropes began to hit the ground, crossing one another in midair and coming down, solid and slowly rhythmic. Cora liked the sound, but she didn't really feel like jumping. Maybe she should have told Zeffy she'd watch. Or turn. That's what she felt like doing—just turning. She wanted to smack those heavy ropes down over and over again, hit hit hit.

Charley was right about Zeffy—her style had improved and her speed too. She looked really good, in fact. Zeffy was smiling at her as she jumped, and Cora smiled back automatically.

> *"I jump East, I jump West,*
> *I jump over the cuckoo's nest.*
> *O-U-T*
> *Out goes me. . . ."*

Zeffy finished, still smiling and not out of breath at all. It was Cora's turn. She hesitated.

"Take your mark, get set," she muttered, and then she was in, letting her legs do it all. No words came to her so she was silent, her shoes thudding against the pavement.

"Knees up," called Zeffy, like Charley did sometimes. "Gotta pick it up."

> *"One two three four five*
> *Cora caught a fish alive. . . ."*

Cora turned her back on Zeffy and sang out, going faster and giving it all she had:

> *"Six seven eight nine ten*
> *Cora let him go again.*
> *Why did she let him go?*
> *Because he bit her finger so. . . ."*

> *"I jump East, I jump West*
> *I jump over the cuckoo's nest.*
> *O-U-T*
> *Out goes me. . . ."*

But she didn't go out as she was supposed to, letting the next girl warm up. She continued to jump, even faster. Zeffy was staring at her, and so were some of the others, but she balled her hands into fists and kept going, faster and faster. She felt her face grow red, but she still couldn't stop. Trees and sky blurred together and her head felt light. She kept on jumping.

She remembered a movie she had once seen called *The Red Shoes*, about a ballerina who danced herself to death. Now that she had started, Cora felt she could easily jump herself to death.

Suddenly, she heard herself reciting in a loud voice, and a moment later, she recognized the words:

> *"Flying man, flying man*
> *Up in the sky,*
> *Where are you going to*
> *Flying so high?*
> *Over the city,*
> *And over the sea*
> *Flying man, flying man*
> *Can't you take me?"*

Over and over again, she repeated the rhyme until it seemed to grow like mold inside her, blackening her heart, which was beating much too hard.

Then, abruptly, she came to a halt and stood there and the ropes died around her, one of them knocking her on the shoulder as it dropped. Hunching over, she tried to catch her breath.

Zeffy approached quietly and waited, and the

other girls waited with her, uneasily.

"Listen," said Cora, when she could finally speak. "Sorry. Hey, I'm not in such good shape today." She smiled apologetically.

"Right," said Zeffy, watching Cora closely. Her eyes looked more lidded than ever.

Cora bent down and picked up a loose pebble, tossing it in the air and catching it a few times. "I'll just turn for a while, okay?" she said. "I really feel like turning."

"You're not gonna jump?" Zeffy asked. "You're just gonna turn?"

"Yeah, that's it," said Cora, picking up the ropes. And frowning fiercely, she began to turn, throwing the heavy ropes up in the air in an arc and letting them hit hit hit. Each time they hit, she felt better somehow, much better.

And then her mother's handwriting floated into her mind, etched and perfectly clear, like giant sky-writing over the Silverpoint beach: *I feel like the steadyender,* Cora read again . . . *like the steadyender.*

12
NIKOS

Cora's mother sat at rigid attention on the living-room couch as if she had been stationed there for weeks. Her cheeks were taut, with rough patches that seemed to be peeling off in little white flakes like paint. Her eyes were crusted and bright pink, like Cora's had been one week when she went on a citrus diet, eating only grapefruit. And she was holding the butterfly note in her hand, crumpling it slightly. She looked exhausted.

Cora stood in the doorway. Finally, she advanced toward her mother. "That's mine," she said quietly, pointing to the aerogramme. "Give it back, please."

Her mother nodded. "I know it's yours, Cora," she said. "I think we should talk about it."

"Why talk about it *now*?" Cora exploded. "You had years to talk about it. At least you could've mentioned it when I asked if he had ever written to me."

"I was hoping to wait until you were older," her mother answered.

"Oh yes, 'old enough to understand,'" Cora quoted angrily. "And when exactly would that be? How old do you need to be to understand that your one and only known parent doesn't tell the truth?" She threw up her hands in a dramatic gesture, but her mother rose and caught them between her own. The letter fell to the floor.

"Just calm down and listen to me, Cora," she said urgently. "You can be angry as long as you like; I'm not going to try and argue you out of it. Maybe I was wrong to wait this long; I don't know. But now that you've read what you have, it's important that you ask me things. . . ." Her mother broke off anxiously as Cora stooped to rescue her father's letter.

Cora remained kneeling, her face averted, tracing the butterfly's journey with her finger. "Okay, I do have a question," she said. "Where are *his* letters? You asked him if he wanted to be my father. He answered, didn't he? I know he did."

Her mother shook her head. "There are some things you're still too young. . ." she began.

"Wouldn't *you* want to know his exact words, if you were me?" Cora broke in indignantly.

"His exact words," her mother echoed bitterly, grimacing. "And how about *this* so-called letter—the only one he ever sent you? What would you say his exact words are, eh? Is this a letter a father sends his daughter? A pretty picture of a butterfly wandering who knows where? The man spoke in riddles. His exact words—yes, his words *were* exact. He was eloquent at times. But he made no sense, no sense at all." And she glared at Cora, who stared back defiantly.

"Eloquent at times?" Cora asked, placing her fingertips together like a television lawyer making a point in court. "Do you know that's the first nice thing you've ever said about him except that he was handsome? There must have been some other things you liked. He was eloquent at times. What else?"

"He was crazy," her mother insisted, frowning.

Cora started to laugh. "Yes, Mom, yes, you've mentioned that. He was crazy. But why did you marry him in the first place, then?"

Her mother shrugged. "Why? Because I was too young to get married, that's why," she said. "Don't cross-examine me, Cora; I don't like it."

"Show me his letters, Mom, please," Cora begged.

Her mother sighed so sadly that Cora almost felt sorry for her. "I wasn't thinking of you when I decided not to save them, Cora" she said softly. "I'm sorry." Cora was silent. "He's not what you imagine," her mother added. "He'd disappoint you."

"Handsome," Cora said. "Eloquent at times. Crazy. Am I on the right track?"

Her mother sighed again and sank back into the couch. She dug at her reddened eyes with her fingers, rubbing them violently. They were both quiet for a minute. "Oh honey, I knew this would come someday, but I don't know where to start," she said miserably, patting a place beside her on the couch.

Cora sat, keeping some distance from her mother. "I could say he was a rat to leave me the way he did, and that's true, I guess. But really, that's not what you want to hear, is it? You asked what I loved about him. Did I ever tell you how we met?"

"In graduate school," Cora said, moving closer and settling in more comfortably. "He was an architect. And you were an art student."

"A photographer," her mother corrected. "I used to work all night in the darkroom while he bent over his drawing board, adding one little line to another."

She hesitated. Cora waited. "I liked the way he handled things when he worked," she continued. "His hands were large, and whatever passed through them seemed improved."

She eyed Cora, pausing again. "He was different from anyone else I knew," she went on. "I mean, we all wanted to invent ourselves in those days. But Nikos never seemed to question his place in the world. I was forever rushing here and there, never even taking time out to sit down to a meal. But Nikos would sit at breakfast a long time, calmly peeling an orange so the skin came off all in one piece. Sometimes, he would take a whole day to chop vegetables for a special soup, just for the two of us. And when we walked together, he would hold my arm and I would find myself matching my pace to his, taking long strides. He slowed me down, made me look around me. . . ." She trailed off.

"So you married him?" Cora prompted.

Her mother shook her head. "Not right away," she said. "First we moved to New York together, and he found a job."

She shook her head again. "He wanted his new boss to know that in Greece, he was heir to his own farm, and that each year it yielded a fine crop of pistachios and figs. He told everyone that in Athens, he had a fishing boat, a car, and a nice house, shaded by lemon trees.

"He wasn't ready for the big city, you see. He was used to people knowing him. At home, everyone knew his family. And as a student, he was talented and had made a name for himself. But he had entered a world of big companies and they didn't know him. They put him in the darkest corner of a vast studio, a space too small for his legs. He took to muttering under his breath. His culture predated theirs by three thousand years, he would say, just loud enough for passersby to hear. His ancestors were carving alabaster statues of the gods while theirs were still in caves chasing skunks with sticks!

"So he was fired. It came as no surprise to me, but it hurt his feelings terribly. . . ."

"And *that's* when you married him?" Cora asked.

"Well, yes," her mother answered. "Yes, that's when I married him. He said he could see ahead to being fired from a second job and a third and a fourth. He felt like a failure."

"You married him to cheer him up?" Cora asked incredulously.

"Not exactly, but, well, it *did* cheer him up, at least for a while." She shrugged. "I knew enough even then to realize you can be very good at something and still fail," she said.

"Like jump rope?" Cora asked pointedly.

"Yes, like jump rope. You can be a star one day and a steadyender the next. And then a star again." Cora nodded, and they locked eyes for a moment.

"Of course, Nikos was right—about the jobs, that

is," said her mother. "He was fired from a few more before he left. But I always felt he just hadn't found his niche. I still think he was a gifted designer."

"Handsome. Eloquent at times. Crazy. A gifted designer," Cora mused. "I guess that all fits together more or less. But not that other part you were talking about. The strong, calm kind of guy that could take his time cooking soup. I can't picture that. That piece doesn't go with the rest. Or with walking on coals, either."

"Remember when you learned to draw lobsters in art class?" her mother asked.

"Yeah. What does that have to do with . . ."

"The teacher put one of them behind a glass pitcher, remember? And she asked you to draw what you saw, not what you *thought* you saw. 'Your mind will say, "That claw should look like a claw,"' she warned, 'but your eye will tell you it's a brown shape, interrupted by a crooked edge. Draw *that* and trust the viewer's brain to put it all together!'"

"So? I don't get it."

"Well, people are different depending on where they are, and who they're with, and what they're doing. . . . We have so many selves, Cora. What I mean is, a claw isn't always a claw. Sometimes it's a brown shape with a crooked edge. But it belongs to the same lobster. . . . Oh dear, I'm not making much sense, am I?"

"No, you're not."

"Okay, you know me as your mom. But then you read those letters and you met another person who's still your mom, but not the familiar one, right? Did all the pieces fit?"

Cora shook her head. "But that's because you kept secrets," she said, suddenly angry again.

"Oh Cora, just think of yourself, for goodness' sakes! Sometimes, you're still my little girl, my baby even. Then off you go with Charley, and you're some kind of social scientist, taking notes on street people. And then sometimes in your head you're an angel's child, the offspring of the gods. Do *those* pieces fit? And how about Charley?"

"Charley?" Cora laughed. "He's just Charley. He has no secrets, at least not from me."

Cora's mother frowned and stood up. She began straightening the magazines on the coffee table.

"Why aren't you taking photographs anymore?" Cora asked suddenly. "Did you stop when I was born?"

"No, before that," her mother answered. She continued to straighten up, smoothing cushions, picking up Cora's jacket and shoes and carrying them to the closet. Cora followed close behind.

"You were an artist," she insisted. "What happened?"

Her mother started to make Cora's bed, then interrupted herself and sat down on the rumpled sheet. "I've been talking too much," she said. "Ask me that another day, Cora. I'm tired now. And you look tired too."

Cora sat down beside her. "Mom?" She pressed all her weight against her mother's arm, as she had when she was a small child and wanted to hear one more chapter of *Pinocchio* before bedtime. Her mother responded as she had then, passing her hand lightly over Cora's hair.

"Cora, Cora . . ." she said. Her voice sounded deeper than usual, and sorrowful. "Honey, I was a mess for months, maybe longer, after Nikos said he wasn't coming back. I couldn't take pictures or read or even think very well. And I couldn't sleep. All I could do was cry.

"Every time I went to take pictures, I felt I was face to face with Nikos. I would look through the lens and there he'd be, larger than life. So I stopped taking pictures. Instead, I went shopping. I never bought anything, I just looked. But there wasn't any little thing about what I *didn't* buy that I could forget. The seams on a shift dress. A field of flowers on a nightgown. The rib weave of a white wool sweater. All those details crammed into my skull and stuck there, as if I was some kind of walking catalogue.

"I would move down the street, talking to myself like one of those crazies you like so much. 'At least I have my brown tweed,' I'd say out loud. 'And my sling-back shoes, at least I still have those. And thank goodness I didn't give away my long cape last spring because it'll come in handy now. But I wonder where I put my khaki coat, and my blazer with gold buttons, and my velvet pants. And where's that turban I wore on Halloween last year?' I couldn't stop taking stock, and going back to start again.

"And then, suddenly, it stopped and I was free. And I stopped crying so much, too. . . ."

Cora studied her mother's face. She had seen her mother cry many times, but it was always over quickly. She couldn't imagine her mooning about for days and talking to herself in the streets like Miss Nancy.

"But you never went back to taking pictures?" she asked.

"No, I never did. You know, when you choose something to photograph, you make a decision. You close off more paths than you follow. I couldn't trust my own choices. I guess I felt I had made some major bad ones in my life, and I didn't want to make any more for a while. I wanted to keep all the paths open. . . . Am I making sense?"

"Sort of. . . . But, Mom, do you still think you made bad choices? I mean, do you wish your life had been different?"

Her mother's face brightened. "No," she said very firmly. "No, I don't," and she grinned. "Do you know why?"

Cora smiled back. "Yeah, I know what you're going to say, but really, is it true? Don't you wish you'd married someone else?"

Her mother reached for her, and they hugged one another hard.

"I had all those regrets until I had you," said her mother. "And then I held you in my arms and I thought, 'This is Cora. Isn't she *something*?' And I knew there'd have been no Cora if my life had been different. I was glad it had all happened just the way it had—because you can't change one part without changing everything." Her mother hugged her again, and Cora let her.

"So," Cora whispered into her mother's shoulder, "if I had grown up with a father, everything else would have been different too. . . ."

"Right," said her mother, breaking away. She

wiped her eyes with her sleeve.

"Like I might not have ever been friends with Charley, for instance . . ." said Cora.

"Right," said her mother again. She looked around Cora's room as if seeing it for the first time through her tears.

"By the way," she asked, after a moment, "where on earth did that *hideous* lamp come from?"

13
MISS NANCY

"You may need professional help," said Charley, shaking his head after Cora had told him about her early-morning meeting with Miss Nancy, "but I'm not sure Lady Moon is the answer."

The two friends were sitting cross-legged on the floor of the shower in Charley's bathroom, whispering even though Charley's mother wasn't home. The stall had a heavy door made out of patterned glass so that no one could see in, and it locked. They had made it their clubhouse for over a year now, decorating the tile with WANTED posters they had printed themselves on Charley's mimeograph machine. At first, Charley's mother had protested, but after a while, she had decided she preferred baths.

"Look, Charley," said Cora earnestly, "I'm not asking you to believe Miss Nancy can really see into the future. I'm just asking you to come with me today."

"Did you know the female platypus is missing from its cage in Bronx Park? At least she *was* missing this morning. Have you heard the news since then?" asked Charley. He had a radio on his lap and was fiddling with the knobs.

Cora reached out and turned it off. "I'd be really scared to do this without you, Charley," she admitted. "Say yes, okay? You'd be better at talking to her, and anyway, don't you want to know the rest of her story?"

"Yeah, I'd like to find out more about her, Cora, but frankly, I'm scared. Do I look like a bodyguard to you? Suppose we get mugged in the halls of the Hotel Riverside? That's not the way I want to make my debut on the eleven o'clock news."

"You're right, Charley, I know you're right." Cora nodded miserably. "But I need to check it out, really I do. Miss Nancy's not the violent type and the neighborhood is by the university, so I bet it's okay. Just run-down, that's all."

"She's not the violent type? You don't read the newspapers, that's your trouble. Lots of mass murderers seem really harmless for years and years until they pop, and then all their neighbors say, 'Oh dear, we never would have guessed. She seemed very nice.'"

"I think Lady Moon's going to tell us something

important, Charley," said Cora.

Charley thought for a moment. "We can't just walk in and sit down and expect her to tell us something important," he protested, after a pause. "We're supposed to have some question to ask her."

Cora grinned victoriously. "It's getting late," she said, standing up suddenly. "And you already know what my question is," she added.

Charley hit his forehead with his fist, rising too. "Is *that* why we're going on this wild goose chase? I thought finding those letters changed things, Cora. Do you still think your dad's going to fly down from Mount Olympus?"

"Not Mount Olympus, no. I don't believe he's a god or an angel anymore. But I still have this feeling I'm going to meet him soon. I don't know exactly when, that's all."

"And Lady Moon is going to tell you?"

"It's worth a try, isn't it?" asked Cora.

The Hotel Riverside was a shambles, but there was a reception desk in the lobby and some normal-looking old ladies sitting around in upholstered chairs. The elevator didn't work, so Cora followed Charley up the ancient staircase to Miss Nancy's room. There was no number 22 on the door, but there was a sign with the hand-lettered motto: WHEN THE SUN IS OUT, WHO REMEMBERS LADY MOON?

"There's still time to back out," Charley said. Cora wedged herself past him and knocked loudly.

A voice from inside called, "It's open. Come in."

In the wavering light, they made out a brass dragon with about a hundred little candles on its back, all of them burning. The smell of incense was strong. "The sweet smell of success," Miss Nancy called, waving them in.

She was sitting on a dilapidated chair, her wide flowered skirt spread out around her. "Glad to meet you," she said to Charley, holding out her hand.

"This is the friend I told you about," said Cora.

"But *she* came for a reading, not me," said Charley, backing up until he was leaning against the wall in the shadows.

Miss Nancy studied him, mowing thin streaks into her lipstick with her front teeth. "Pity," she said. "You're easier." And she continued to look Charley over.

Charley crossed his arms over his chest. There was an awkward silence.

Finally, Miss Nancy let out a hoarse bark that sounded something like a laugh. "Did you want to know why I like pigeons? Dalton, my husband, *he* liked them, that's why," she said. "I don't like them much myself. But Dalton, yes, he raised them. Rollers and tumblers. One kind had fancy feathers on their legs and the other did spins—high dives and do-si-dos. Sometimes, I'd get dizzy, trying to keep track of them. Then one would get tired and pass out and fall, just like that. Down it would go, with no warning. 'All part of Nature's plan,' Dalton would say. *'The paper is still while the pen writes,'* he'd say. 'Remember that.'"

Miss Nancy examined her dirty fingernails as if they held an important message she was trying to decode. "And that's what happened to him, too," she added. "Just got tired and down he went, with no warning."

She gazed into Charley's eyes. "First his nails turned purple and he couldn't see. Then pains in his chest." She blinked slowly. "You've seen some of it yourself," she said, searching Charley's face.

"Seen what?" he asked, turning pale.

"Sickness," she answered. She leaned over to him, lightly brushing his eyes with the back of her hand. He jerked away from her touch, then glanced over at Cora as if she could rescue him. Cora stared back at him, bewildered.

"We never do guess the end from the beginning,

Charley. Remember that," said Miss Nancy softly. "Dalton wasn't sick a day in his life till he was sick every day. Went a little crazy in the end, like your dad. But that's not what you came to Lady Moon to hear." She rose and came close to Charley, placing heavy hands on his shoulders. This time, he didn't move.

"My father wasn't ever crazy," he whispered hoarsely. "He was a soldier. He was shot."

"I see a man," she said firmly. "He's very thin, too thin, and he's doing something. What's he doing? Eating apples, he's eating apples, that's what. But he won't finish them, no, he takes one real bite and leaves the rest. . . .

"What now? He's in a bed, near a window, and he's lining up those apples with one bite missing on the sill. There they all are, gnawed and mulchy. They're staining the paint, but he doesn't care. He starts counting, pointing to each one and giving it a number. One two three four five six . . . and then he runs out of apples but he keeps on counting . . . seven eight nine. . ."

"*Charley!*" Cora cried. Charley had flung Miss Nancy aside and opened the door, heading down the hall. Hurriedly, Cora took a five-dollar bill from her purse and held it out to the clairvoyant, though she wasn't sure she was supposed to offer money. Miss Nancy waved it away.

Cora fled then, chasing after Charley, who had disappeared down the stairs. She ran outside, her jacket flapping wildly. Charley wasn't anywhere in sight. Panicking, she veered around and there he was, in the middle of the block. She yelled his name. He turned and waited for her to catch up, but his eyes were half shut and he looked ill.

"I can't believe this," she panted as she came close. "Were you just going to disappear on me?"

He nodded, not speaking.

"What happened in there?" she demanded. "Why did you run away?" He shrugged.

"There's a newsstand over there," he said hoarsely. "I'll be back in a minute."

She watched him buy a paper, then, waving to her, he sat down on a bench to wait for the bus. Spreading the newspaper out across his lap, he bent over it, clasping his hands under his chin.

"Bamboo is the oldest living gorilla in captivity," he said when she sat down next to him. "Says here he's got some kind of chronic stomach problem. They can't tell if its psychosomatic." He turned the page.

"Do you know how weird you're acting, Charley?" Cora asked. "Tell me what's going on, okay?"

Charley started rattling the paper in front of his face. "Ever hear of the subway fold?" he asked. "It's good citizenship. We learned it in fourth grade, but I think you were absent that day. To prevent disturbing your neighbors on a bus or train, you practice origami with *The New York Times* like this—watch." And he held up one section, folding it in half lengthwise and then in half again. "But it's very time-consuming," he said, folding it again. He started tearing off pages, crumpling them in his hand and throwing them on the sidewalk. "It has to be done just right. . . ."

Cora watched him. "Do you think you're being funny?" she asked after a moment.

"No."

"What then? "

"I'm being crazy, Cora. Just like my dad was before he died. Didn't you hear what Miss Nancy said? My dad went a little crazy in the end."

"Was that true?"

"Yes, everything she said was absolutely accurate. He was that man she was talking about—the apple man. He'd take one bite and leave the rest lined up on the sill, just like she said. And he'd throw tea bags at the ceiling too, so their leaves would burst out and drop on the rug. One time, he asked me for a grapefruit, and then he mashed it into his own face so that all the juice dripped out on the sheets. If you'd stayed, you might have heard all about that."

"So he wasn't shot through the heart?" said Cora slowly.

"I made that up," Charley answered miserably. "My father had a brain tumor. It took him months to die."

"And the ladies?" asked Cora.

"What ladies?"

"The ones made out of bullets in your room?"

"I bought them in a flea market. They're from Israel, I think."

"So you lied," Cora whispered.

Charley turned away from her, scanning the traffic.

"I can't believe this," Cora said again, clenching her fists. "Here I was talking and talking about my father, and you deliberately kept what you know about yours a *secret*. My mother was right. Your pieces don't fit either. And all along, I thought you told me *everything*."

Charley whirled around and faced her. "I'm glad I never told you!" he yelled. "I was afraid you'd be like this if I did, that's why. All you can think about is that I kept something from *you*. Your mom kept something from *you*. My dad was very sick," he said, starting to cry. "He *wanted* to die. If I'd told you that, I'd have to remember it; don't you understand anything?"

Suddenly, Cora did understand. And in the same moment, she understood her mother better too. It wasn't just that she had thought it best to wait until Cora was older before showing her those letters. It wasn't only Cora she had been protecting, it was herself. "I couldn't read, or take pictures, or even think very well," her mother had said. "And I couldn't sleep. All I could do was cry." Why should she want to remember all that? It sounded awful. And what Charley had been through sounded even worse. Cora touched Charley's hand, but he shook her off.

"I'm sorry," she whispered. "I'm sorry I even brought you here. It's all my fault."

"Forget it," he mumbled. "Let's just forget it." But she knew neither of them would.

"Miss Nancy is the last one," Cora said suddenly. "I mean, no more crazies from now on, right?"

"Unless your father *does* show up," said Charley.

Cora blinked, stunned into silence. "That's not kind," she said after a moment.

They sat, not speaking, until the bus drew up and they boarded, Cora tripping clumsily on the steps. It was crowded, so they had to take seats across the aisle from one another. Usually, when that happened, they clowned around and made faces, but this time, Charley kept his eyes averted. Cora worked at keeping back her tears.

When the woman next to her got off, Charley stood up and came over. Cora expected him to sit beside her, but he just hung on to the bar, staring out the window above her head, not saying a word for the entire trip uptown.

14
CHARLEY

Cora could not remember the exact chain of events that had ended with her being on the train, bound for Silverpoint, with Charley's big lamp, wrapped up in plastic, sitting on the seat beside her. But the early part of the morning was clear in her mind.

Upon waking, she had eagerly opened the box that contained a new pair of sneakers for the jump rope tournament that day. And she had found, to her dismay, that it held two for the same foot.

"Bad luck," she had announced to her mother. "I have two left feet!"

"Didn't you try them on?" her mother asked.

"No," Cora admitted. "They were exactly the same as my old ones, only white."

"Well, you'll just have to wear your old ones, then," her mother said, shrugging.

"This is an omen," Cora complained. "I bet if I

looked at my chart today, the stars would be telling me to stay home. I'm glad *you're* not coming at least. It'll be embarrassing enough when I lose without having you there in the stands feeling sorry for me."

Cora's mother looked hurt. "I don't know why I let you convince me not to come this time," she said, frowning. "I've never missed it before. I like seeing you out there with all the other kids."

Dressing quickly, Cora unfolded a brand-new shirt, and a small slip of paper dropped out. "Folded by Four, Inspected by Eleven," she read. "Who's Four and who's Eleven?" she wondered, pulling on her jeans.

The question continued to bother her as she combed her hair in front of the bathroom mirror. Four was married, but had no children, she decided. Eleven was a teenager and still lived with her parents—or maybe just her mother. They both hated their boring jobs at the shirt factory. She wished Charley was there—he could have provided a long and complicated history for each of them.

She had thought of calling him the night before to find out for certain if he was coming, but then she had decided against it. They hadn't spoken since the day they had consulted Lady Moon, but she couldn't imagine him missing the tournament.

"I'll just look for his bicycle," she thought. It was impossible to miss, even in a crowd, because it had a frizzy yellow wig as a seat cover, several large rubber frogs hanging from the handlebars, and endangered species stickers all over the chrome.

But suppose he didn't show up? She had to admit, it was a possibility.

"Are you still getting ready?" asked her mother, popping her head into Cora's room. "I'm running out to do a little shopping, Cora. See you when you get back. Good luck, honey," and she popped back out again. Cora heard the front door slam.

She was alone by her own choice, but still, it felt as if she'd been abandoned. She sat down abruptly on her bed. Why was she forcing herself to go through with this thing? Zeffy was going to win, and no one she cared about would be there anyway. She remembered the day she had been the steadyender with Zeffy. Her cheeks grew hot with humiliation, and she pressed her arms into her sides. She was moving toward that miserable state her mother called a worry trance.

To dispel it, she stood up purposefully and walked over to her bookshelf, tracing her finger along the bindings until she reached the encyclopedia. Absently, she stroked the gold letters, then taking down the E volume, opened to "Europa."

". . . a maiden loved by Zeus," she read. *"Disguised as a handsome white bull, he mingled with her father's cattle and tempted her to climb on his back. Then he charged into the sea and carried her to Crete, where he gave her three gifts: a bronze man to guard the island, a hunting hound that never lost the scent, and a spear that never missed its mark. Later, the presents were passed along to their son, King Minos."*

What gifts had her father ever given her? Cora mused. A birdcage minus a bird, a bunch of neckties, and a mobile made out of junk.

She turned back to the open page, to a painting like the one in her long ago dream, except that it was in black and white. There was Europa herself, in a transparent robe, draped across the bull's broad back and gazing serenely into a bright sky. The beast's horns were adorned with flowers. "She doesn't look too upset," Cora observed.

Moving to her desk, she played with some colored pencils in a coffee can, jiggling them so that they made a hollow sound, until her hand came to rest on one. She pressed the tip, and a silvery dust came off on her skin.

Slowly, she bent over the book again so that her hair brushed the page and lightly, lightly she touched the bull's flowers with the point of her silver pencil. A shock of pleasure went through her.

She pressed a little harder, burying all the blossoms in a silvery gray. As she watched them blur and disappear, she had the urge to kiss them good-bye, one by one.

Then, starting on the bull himself, slowly, methodically, she built a beautiful silver mist, layer by layer. And then she let it spread to Europa too, and to the sky, until the whole picture dissolved into a small square of fog, blotting god and goddess out of existence. As she worked, the tight knot in her chest loosened and she started to relax. And when she was finished, her handiwork shimmered at her, like a patch cut from the tinfoil wings of the angel on the library steps.

The thought of the library brought her back to earth. She had never marked a book before, never, even when she was very small. Suddenly, she felt like a criminal, and the ruined illustration stared up at her accusingly. Quickly, she turned the page, but the paper was so crisp from the pressure she had exerted that it snapped. She slammed the book shut and replaced it on the shelf.

The moment she slipped it into place, she knew, as clearly as if he had called to tell her so, that Charley wouldn't be at the tournament. And she knew she wouldn't be either. She turned and stared at Charley's lamp, finding it even uglier than when he had first brought it over. Typical of Charley to think it had magic powers, when it was just ordinary and not even very nice.

The notion came to her that she should get rid of it somehow, set it afloat like a giant bottle in the ocean. Maybe it would find its way to some Greek island, to a child who had lost a father. To Baubo maybe—she might be real after all.

Now that she had decided Charley wasn't going to show up, she was angry enough at him to send the lamp to sea without asking him first. It was really her lamp—he had given it to her, and that meant she could do whatever she wanted with it. She pictured it at sea, bobbing ridiculously on a towering wave, and she smiled, relieved and almost happy for the first time that morning.

But now that she was actually on the train, with the unwieldy bundle on the seat beside her, a more solemn mood had set in.

A poster on the wall just in front of her showed two people sharing cocktails, but the photograph, which was very large, included only their torsos and hands and not their heads. Seeing parts of people in pictures always disturbed her, especially if their heads were missing. Her mother told her she would point to them, even as a baby, wherever they appeared, demanding the picture to be whole.

She thought of what her mother had said the other day about how, most of the time, pieces don't all fit together but the person who's looking at them provides the missing links. She closed her eyes, trying to imagine the poster showing the couple's faces. But just as with Four and Eleven, the details wouldn't come. Again, she felt a sharp pang, wishing Charley was beside her. "Let's see," he would say, "the girl has kind of a weak chin with maybe a witch wart on it, tiny but noticeable. And the guy is Wall Street all the way."

Cora opened her eyes. Sitting directly under the poster was an obese woman, taking up nearly two seats. Cora wondered how she would feel if she were that fat. Change one thing, and you change everything, she told herself, echoing her mother again. If she was fat, would she still be Cora? No, not really. She'd be fat Cora and she didn't remotely know what that was like.

If she was fat Cora, maybe she would have a father. But if she had a father, would she be happier, even though she was fat? Just because you have a father doesn't mean you're happy. She knew that from Zeffy, who didn't like her dad much. "Just because you have legs doesn't mean you can walk," Charley had said one time. "Take the dragonfly, for instance. It has six legs but it doesn't walk at all. And if it did walk, would it fly?"

Cora shook herself impatiently. All her thoughts kept coming back to Charley. She couldn't seem to keep her mind on anything without summoning him.

She had wanted to tell him so many things on the way home from Miss Nancy, but he had acted so angry she hadn't dared. There was this odd graffiti they passed just as they got off the bus. It said: INVISIBILITY IS YOUR REVENGE in huge airbrush letters. It had made her think of her invisible dad. Maybe it was her dad's revenge against her mother to be invisible. It was the kind of thing she would usually have discussed with Charley at length, but he had marched by the message, pretending not to notice, so she had too. And now Charley was being invisible.

"Siiillverpoiint!" The conductor called it out with more enthusiasm than he had the other stops. Cora lurched down the aisle and out the doors, balancing her bulky package with difficulty. She looked around the station as the train pulled away, searching for someone who could give her directions to the ocean. The place was desolate, as densely gray and featureless as the obliterated painting she had left at home in the encyclopedia.

At the far end of the platform, a man with grease spots on his trousers sat huddled on a bench, drinking coffee from a paper cup.

"Excuse me," she said, approaching. "I'm sorry to bother you, but could you tell me . . ."

He turned his face to her, and she saw there were spots in his eyes as well as on his pants and they seemed to be moving around, circumnavigating his eyeballs. "The beach is three blocks that way," he interrupted her, pointing to the right. "You walk straight as the gull flies, past the parking lot, past the gas station, past the Stop and Shop, past the hot dog stand, past the fire hydrant, past the video store, past the wax museum, and up a ramp to the boardwalk and down seven and a half steps." He nodded and took another sip of coffee.

"Thank you," said Cora, but it was only after she had taken the last seven and a half steps down to the sand that it dawned on her that the man was blind. The heavy lamp was making her arms ache, but she didn't want to set it down yet. She decided to walk along until she reached a place that seemed right. Then she'd bury the lamp and go for a long hike—and maybe visit the aquarium.

She had been to the aquarium a few times with her mother, and the sight of the white whales, strong and sleek, swimming gracefully in their turquoise tank, always made her feel good. The two belugas seemed like the only well-matched married pair she knew about, always kissing and rubbing noses in the water.

Cora scanned the area to get her bearings, looking for the Ferris wheel. She saw it, shining in the distance, utterly empty and still. Though the sky was overcast, the light was strong. She blinked, sucking the salty air and dampness deep into her lungs.

Gulls were evenly spaced out along the wide stretch of sand, standing very still, like shooting-gallery targets. A race walker passed by, pumping her arms and striding stiffly. As she lugged the lamp farther, Cora noticed that the few people out were all exercising.

Up ahead, a muscular man with white tape around his ankles was swinging a baseball bat and doing a kind of hopping dance, back and forth, near the waves, like a boxer before placing a punch. And farther along, a woman in a neon yellow leotard was coiling and uncoiling like a snake to amplified sounds of the surf on a tape recorder that looked in danger of being carried away by the surf itself.

Cora sat down on a rock that sheltered a tiny tide pool and watched a thin red worm doing a continuous figure eight in its corner of sea water. In fifth grade, she used to do the same drawing over and over again—a looping group of figure eights (Charley had said they represented infinity) which she'd fill with spectacular colors, thickly applied before covering them even more thickly in black crayon. Then she'd scratch out one thin agitated line, dramatically multicolored, with her fingernail.

The memory brought her back to the more recent experience of coloring Europa and her bull silver. Why had she done it? she asked herself, as she watched the worm. It was definitely a weird thing to do.

She sighed and, shouldering her burden, continued down the beach, stumbling a bit. She had reached the cabanas. They all looked abandoned, but there was a noisy group of gulls in one of them, flapping and flying in and out of the doorway as if beckoning her to hurry over.

Suddenly, Cora felt tired. Convinced she couldn't carry the lamp another step, she dropped it right where she stood. The garbage bag protecting it split open, and Cora felt a surge of disgust. How could she ever have believed in the stupid old thing? It was just what it looked like—garbage fit for the dump. She had truly thought, when she had first knelt before it on that rainy night, that it would speak. She had really imagined it could tell her about her father. It was all nothing but Charley's hocus-pocus, and she had been dumb enough to believe it.

She began to drag the lamp unceremoniously by its fraying shade toward the water, cutting a broad and winding furrow in the soft sand. When she reached firmer ground, she planted it like an umbrella, sculpting a shallow ridge around its base so it would stand upright. It cast a clear shadow. She was casting a very sharp-edged shadow now too, she noticed, though the sky was still banked with heavy clouds, like slabs of silver granite blocking the sun.

Another morning on the beach came back to her, a windy walk when she was very young, when her mother had taken a stick and, stooping down, had carefully traced Cora's shadow in the wet sand and then her own. The two shadows, side by side, had filled Cora with a happiness, so perfect and resounding that she had taken her mother's face in both hands and gazed at her for one long moment before throwing her arms wide and running at top speed down the beach.

She began to run now, away from the lamp and its shadow, and the farther she got, the lighter and swifter she felt until she almost tripped over a young boy, lying asleep, his head resting in the center of his bicycle's front wheel. The glowing spokes seemed to radiate from his face, and she gazed at him in a kind of rapture for a while. Then she backed away, glad she hadn't disturbed him. As she looked up at the sky, the Ferris wheel, much closer now, caught a shaft of slate blue light and glistened like a giant echo of the boy's steely pillow.

She wasn't far from the aquarium, and she headed straight for it, into the salty wind that seemed to be stronger the closer she came to the boardwalk. A garish Paul Bunyan, his giant feet firmly planted in the midget golf course, pointed the way with his ax like an oversized signpost.

"Free day," said the cashier, smiling encouragingly and raising her eyebrows. Cora hurried inside the building, past two big gray fish eating sand, over to where she had last seen the belugas, but to her dismay, they were gone. She retraced her steps and checked the schedule posted on the wall. The whales were about to perform in the marine mammal theater.

Cora followed a few stragglers out to the stands that encircled a pool where two sea lions were acting like clowns, applauding the audience with their flippers. She hunched into the stiff breeze, waiting for the whales to make their entrance, but the show seemed to go on and on.

She glanced over the fence at the penguins down below. There was another group of people gathered there, and the keeper was lecturing, informing them of the mating habits of penguins in the wild. "By the time the female lays her eggs," he was saying, "she's gone two or three weeks without eating. So she takes off to find a meal while the father squats down on the eggs. And he just stays there, no matter how cold it gets, through one-hundred-mile-an-hour blizzards, even if his feet freeze, until the mother returns."

"Good thing I'm not a penguin," Cora thought. "I never would have made it out of the egg."

Cora turned her attention back to the show. Ah, the belugas had finally come out, and their trainer was blowing on a whistle. "What do you say when people call you a fish?" she asked one of them.

"*Phhhutt!*" said the whale into a microphone.

Cora pulled her jacket tighter. It was getting too cold to stand still outside. She retreated back into the main hall and found herself staring into the manatee's tank, but it was being shy, refusing to turn its head and look at her. All she could see was its paddlelike tail. She remembered seeing its face the last time she was there—with a flat, piggish nose and huge nostrils flaring as it breathed—but today, though she waited awhile, it never acknowledged her.

Finally, she gave up and entered a hall labeled BERMUDA TRIANGLE. The Bermuda Triangle—isn't that where airplanes and things disappear? she asked herself. She wondered if Charley would just disappear and never want to see her again. Maybe *she* should just disappear, and then it would be Charley who was left feeling lonely.

She read the sign over the turtle tank. "*Turtles have been around for three hundred million years,*" it said. These turtles didn't look that ancient, though. Their shells weren't dented and blistered and shaggy with seaweed but clean, like brushed teeth. And their pinpoint eyes were alert under heavy lids. Again Charley's voice intruded. Turtles were one of his causes.

"Did you know that tourists are worse for the turtles than all the fire and ice and floods in history?" he had asked her once. "See, baby turtles are programmed to head for the light after they're born. There's only one small problem. The light used to be the horizon line. Now guess where they end up. In the hotel lobbies, waiting for the elevators!"

Cora thought she recalled having a dream about

a turtle, then realized with a start that it wasn't her dream at all, but the disturbing one Charley had told her when he had given her the lamp. Not only was she hearing his voice at every turn, but she was even mixing up his dreams with her own!

She turned and strode out of the aquarium, heading for the open air. What should she do now? She could go home, but she probably wasn't even due back from the tournament yet, and she wasn't sure if she wanted to tell her mother about missing it. Maybe she should just run again and try to shake Charley out of her system.

She couldn't believe how much she had been missing him all day. As she walked toward the ocean, she thought of her mother's letter.

I no longer walk down the street feeling tipped off balance because your arm isn't around me. It must have been terrible for her mother to have someone that close and then never see him again.

She understood better now why her mother had told Nikos he had to be a father all the time or not at all. In a way, she was glad she had never known her father, so that she didn't have to remember him after he left.

Life leads where it leads, her mother had told her. It had led her father away from her. Maybe it was best that way. Close up, he might not be anything like what she had imagined. Anyway, she couldn't waste her life just expecting him to come. Either he would or he wouldn't, and that was that.

Her hair whipped into her mouth and she pulled it out, grimacing. Her thoughts turned to Charley again. Poor Charley. After his father died, he must have been hearing his father's voice all the time, not just when he talked to the lamp. At the thought of the lamp, she looked toward it, squinting into the wind. She shouldn't have left it in the middle of the beach. By now, it had probably been blown down and away.

But no, it was still there—someone was standing beside it. Cora let out a yell and began to run, kicking up clouds of sand as she went. Charley turned the way a man on a picket line would, his body stiff as a sandwich board. Then he saw her and waved, with a sudden grin that grew like a vine pruned slightly too much on one side. The light had turned pure gold now, like a thousand jars of honey. It lit a halo around his hair. She galloped up to him and just stood there, panting. The wind took what was left of her breath away and dusted her face with sand.

"In the craters of the moon, dust particles are so small they stay in the air for months after the wind stops," said Charley. "Or is it Mars?"

She opened her mouth to answer but nothing came out, and she thought of the tale her mother used to tell her of the mermaid who sold her tongue for love. She pictured the poor changeling girl, speechless, looking out over the waves. Say hello, she told herself, but instead she yawned. Then she blushed, tossing her head like a horse trying to rid itself of flies. What was wrong with her? She yawned again.

Charley laughed. "In 1888, a girl about our age yawned nonstop for six weeks. It set a record," he said.

"You doggy dog, you didn't call me!" she blurted, punching him in the arm.

"Well, I showed up at the tournament, which is more than you did," he answered. "Zeffy was pretty disappointed, you know."

Cora shrugged. "I don't care about Zeffy," she said, twisting her foot into the sand. "I didn't think you'd come to the tournament," she added after a pause.

"Would I miss it? Never! I'm your coach, don't forget. Or I was."

Charley looked away toward the cabanas, suddenly awkward. "I knew you'd be here," he said. Cora didn't answer. "I didn't know you'd walk so *far*, though," he added. "I almost gave up until I saw the lamp."

They both stared at the lamp and fell silent. Finally, Cora said, "I missed you."

"Yeah, me too."

They continued to watch the lamp, as if it would flash them a signal of what to do next.

"It was weird seeing it here," said Charley.

"I wanted to send it out to sea," Cora explained. "To Greece maybe. Like a bottle, but without a message."

"It's okay," said Charley. "I don't mind. It was just weird, that's all. For a second, I forgot I had given it to you. It freaked me out to see it, half-buried there in the sand."

"Sorry," she said, and surprised herself by taking his hand. But it was clenched into a fist. She looked at him questioningly and he opened his palm, revealing the twin bullet ladies, clinking against one another. Cora stared at them. She had never noticed the shiny lines and triangles decorating their bellshaped skirts. Even the tiny jug one of them held on her head was patterned.

"Take them," said Charley, watching her. "Why don't you keep them?" He let the two dolls roll into her hand, and she closed her fingers over them. They felt weighty, like anchors giving her a welcome balance in the wind.

She remembered wishing Charley would give her this very present for her birthday but knowing he would never part with them. So much had changed since then. She had felt then that if she owned the two souvenirs of Charley's dad, her own father would surface, like a wily old fish that had long avoided the hook. And like sinkers on a deep-sea fishing line, they would help her reel him in. But she was no longer sure she really wanted to find her father. It might be better if he never showed up at all.

Still, she was happy to have the bullets, and even happier that Charley had given them to her. He hadn't disappeared—and he never would; she knew that now.

She looked up at him, suddenly shy. "Thanks, Charley," she whispered. But he was staring out to sea.

A great green wave had appeared on the horizon— larger than any that had preceded it—and it was progressing toward them smoothly, like a towering parade float. They watched, fascinated, as it broke with tremendous force, then seethed toward them, erasing the tide line. Charley took her arm and pulled her backward as the cold frothy water drenched their feet.

"My shoe!" shrieked Cora. Standing on one leg to grab the loose one before it came off in the surf, she toppled backward, sending Charley crashing down too as he continued to drag her away.

"Oh no," they moaned together, but the water was already receding and they weren't terribly wet. They started to laugh, then watched as the amazing wave, showing its superior strength even in retreat, lifted Charley's lamp and carried it away.

Bumping and rolling on the current that had captured it, the lamp seemed to be waving good-bye and Cora waved back. Then Charley did too, laughing. And their combined laughter made them roll from side to side on the wet sand, as if they, like the lamp, had been kidnapped by a surprisingly strong tide.

15
THE BULL

That night, Cora dreamed she was swimming among a congregation of lily pads in a pond. Suddenly, she saw what looked like a corpse, floating in the water just ahead. Weeds and rushes partially hid it from view, but she glimpsed the twist of a rope looped like pastry around its neck, and a doily of froth laced with leaves blocking its mouth. A dragonfly flickered over the dark bruises on its skin, which gleamed, pale as a marble pedestal. Vines obscured the rest.

She came closer and realized it was not a man, as she had feared at first, but a large—no, a monumental—white bull.

16
THE CRAZY'S DAUGHTER

"What is it you like about Cootie?" asked Cora, watching Charley as he carefully set out the little brightly colored plastic body parts on the board. "It's really for babies, isn't it?"

"You aren't backing out, are you, Cora?" Charley asked. "Because you know you've been promising to play this with me for a long time now."

"I know, I know," Cora said. "It looks kind of simple, that's all. I mean, compared to the other games you like," she added.

"Maybe I just like these silly smiling bugs," said Charley, throwing her a sideways glance. "Or the fact that all *these* pieces fit."

"Give me a break," said Cora.

"Well, they do," Charley insisted, lining them all up on their corresponding pictures very precisely. "And there's an order that makes perfect sense. You have to have a body and a head before you can try for anything else, like eyes or antennae. I mean, it's all in the roll of the dice but still . . . it's basic."

"So is washing the dishes, but it's not very interesting."

"Oh, but it *can* be, especially if you stack them right."

"Yeah, I know your technique on that score, Charley. You pile them all up so that the first move to dry them brings them down."

Charley nodded and continued to work on his arrangement of yellow Cootie legs. "Okay, we're set now. Let's throw the dice to see who goes first."

"You can go first," said Cora, yawning.

"No, whoever gets the higher number," said Charley. "You can't go changing the rules."

"Mom better come back with the pizza soon," said Cora. "I'm starved." She leaned her elbows on the kitchen table and bent her head toward the toaster, examining herself in the shiny chrome. Her reflection looked swollen, her nose resembling a pig's snout. For an instant she felt disoriented, and in that instant, the doorbell rang and she heard a shuffling in the hall.

"Your turn," said Charley. "Is that your mother?"

"She has a key," said Cora, slipping from her chair and moving to the spy hole. She peered out at a stranger and just had time to notice how tall he was before her mother appeared, climbing laboriously up the stairs with their lunch. Cora watched as the two froze and stared at one another.

"My God!" said the man. But her mother said nothing, just stood there, breathing.

"What's happening?" Charley whispered. Cora shook her head, shushing him.

"Ask me in?" she heard the man say. Her mother still didn't move. Finally, she began fumbling in her handbag, looking for her keys. Cora took that as a signal to open the door. At the sight of Cora's face, her mother thrust the pizza box at Charley and drew Cora toward her.

"My, my," said the visitor, studying the three of them. "Is this possible? Is this really possible?" His glance kept shifting from Cora to Charley to her mother again.

His eyes were black, as dark as the abysmal drop Cora saw sometimes just before sleep, when she imagined she had lost her footing and was falling down a precipice. His triangular eyebrows looked like two thunderclouds, penciled graffiti-style on his skin. And he was bald.

Her mother let out a long, jagged sigh. "Cora, this is your father, Nikos," she announced. And to him she said, recovering slightly, "This is Cora's friend, Charley. We're about to have . . . pizza. . . ."

She trailed off into silence and they all stood looking at one another.

Charley put the pizza down. "Nice to meet you, sir," he said, bowing formally. "When you rang, Cora and I were just playing Cootie. I was winning. We'd have time for one more round, if you'd like to join us." He sat down cross-legged at the table next to the game board and patted the place beside him. "I used to play this with *my* father," he added reassuringly.

Nikos looked at Cora's mother and shrugged. "Okay?" he asked.

Cora couldn't believe that her father was suddenly there, about to sit beside Charley at their kitchen table, about to play Cootie and eat pizza. And just when she had given up on him. It was too strange. He didn't look anything like a Greek god either. He had deep lines in his forehead and around his mouth, giving him a troubled look. Her mother had said he was handsome but he just looked old to her.

Cora glanced at her mother and found her glaring at Nikos.

"I'm staying in New York for a little while," he said, rubbing his knees awkwardly.

"So you decided to drop in?" Her mother placed

dark emphasis on the last two words. "Why didn't you call?"

"Would you have let me come?" he asked, meeting her eyes.

"*I've* been expecting you ever since my birthday," Cora spoke up, surprising herself. "I knew you'd come soon, I just didn't know exactly when. Ask Charley, if you don't believe me."

Her father's face opened into a dazzling smile. Suddenly, he did look handsome.

"I read your letter," she continued, blushing.

He looked confused. "My letter?"

"Don't you remember?" she asked urgently. "The one with the butterfly?"

"The butterfly, yes," he said, looking away.

He stood up, walking over to a shelf on which Cora's pottery was displayed. He dusted it with his finger.

"So you're an artist, eh?" he asked, changing the subject. "Like your mother."

"No, I'm just in an art club after school," she answered.

Solemnly, he picked out a round blue pot and held it in his large hand, as if weighing it on a scale of justice. He replaced it carefully and studied the other pieces, taking his time. Finally, he chose a large vase in the shape of a rooster, its beak curled like an autumn leaf, its middle pinched and its tail puffed beyond barnyard pride. He displayed it on his arm, turning it around and around.

"Look at that line," he exclaimed, tracing the bird's bulging neck. "Look how firmly those legs are planted in the earth." They were so thick, they had fused together in the kiln. "This rooster is bold, natural. . . ."

He went on praising it from all angles, and Cora could have sworn that the crippled fowl straightened out under his scrutiny, correcting its unfortunate spinal twist. She became convinced that she had fashioned a prize fighting cock. A wave of gratitude rose in her throat.

"Thank you," she said, turning a deep scarlet. She fixed her gaze on her father's monumental jaw, which was rippling with tension. She wanted to register his every move, his slightest gesture.

He nodded, replacing the vase, and sat down again at the table. He seemed too big for the chair. Rubbing the deep creases in his forehead, he winked at Cora. "Cora Eve, Cora Eve," he chanted, as if testing the name. "Do you always muster such a glow? I can feel the heat from here," and he lifted his clenched hands and slowly opened them, leaning toward his daughter as if toward a friendly flame. She reddened even more.

"Let's eat," her mother broke in. "I'm sure everyone's hungry. Charley, why don't you gather up that unattractive toy, and Cora, help me set out the plates."

Cora had almost forgotten Charley was there. She was relieved to see him fumbling around with his nonsensical insects. Her breathing was coming in scattered little puffs, and her lungs ached. She set out the silverware with a clatter.

"Where are you staying?" asked her mother as she poured out some soda.

"In SoHo," he answered, "with a girl I met at a firewalk. Chelsea's her name."

"Chelsea?"

"She came right up to me in Central Park and admired my feet." Nikos laughed. "They're so large, she told me, and smooth as ice. 'They give me courage.'" He laughed again, shrugging. "It was her first stroll across the coals, you see," he explained. "She was scared, of course."

"Of course," said her mother, trying to catch Cora's eye.

Cora lifted her face and blinked, her pizza suspended in midair. So it was true, he *did* walk on coals! Firewalk, he had said. He was a firewalker.

Suddenly, she saw him as an intruder, as unwelcome as the Mushroom would be if he invited himself to a meal in their home. He looked untrustworthy, like a frog preparing to hunt for flies by blending in with the camouflaging marsh grass. He had seemed okay when he first walked in, but here he was talking about firewalks. Again, she heard Charley's comment that day on the way home from Miss Nancy. No more crazies, she had said. And he had answered, "Unless your father *does* show up."

"You may laugh," Nikos was saying, "but it works, it really does. Do you know how hot those hot coals get? Two thousand degrees. They roll steel at two thousand degrees. I tell you, Sara, when you've braved the burning embers, you can do anything. Anything. It can't be described. I can't come close to describing it."

"Don't try then," said her mother, smiling slightly.

Cora felt dizzy. She nudged Charley's foot under the table. His shoelaces were untied as usual. He hadn't said a word this whole time. What was he thinking? He was playing with the food on his plate, supporting his head with one hand and listlessly pushing large cheesy pieces around. He looked like he was about to take a nap right there.

"Are you happy with Chelsea?" her mother was asking. But Cora wasn't sure she had really heard the question correctly.

"You haunt me," her father answered. "You both do, you know."

Their voices sounded so far away. Cora was having trouble hearing.

"I'd say it was the other way around," her mother answered. "For some reason, you've come here to haunt us."

"I won't trouble you, Sara," he promised. "I just wanted to see her this once."

"This once?" asked Cora faintly, but she was having as much difficulty hearing her own voice as the others'. Though she remained motionless, she felt as if she were pushing back in her chair. The walls, she noticed, were growing dim, the outlines of her parents sitting uncomfortably side by side, barely discernible in the fading light. The only thing that kept its shape was Charley's face, which she saw very clearly. Desperately, she touched his arm.

"I guess you won," she said, pointing to the Cootie game.

"Yeah, but next time, you'll know all the rules," he said charitably.

"I can hear Charley okay," she thought with some relief. She tried to answer him but it was like trying to swallow something too big for her mouth.

Bending over, as if to study the floor, she started to shudder uncontrollably. All her dreams from the last few weeks came crowding into her head—the bald sea captain in the boat bound for Greece, the faceless man with binoculars who had danced with her, and the white bull, drowned among the lily pads. Tears dripped down, staining her dress.

"Cora?" her mother cried out, rising.

Distinctly, Cora heard the destructive roar of heavy storm winds and the grinding of an iron gate—the Silverpoint gate. And before her mother could rush to her side, she caved in, collapsing into Charley's outstretched arms as the gate slammed shut, barring entrance to her father, the crazy who walked on coals. And to Cora Eve Pavlides—the crazy's daughter.

17
LADY MOON

When Cora came to, it was dark, and her father and Charley had gone. Her mother was sitting by her bedside, and Cora could feel her presence even before opening her eyes. "I'm okay," she murmured, and she turned over, facing the wall. "Here I wait twelve years for my father to show up, and when he does, I faint. What did Charley have to say?"

"He was worried, that's all."

"I made a fool of myself," said Cora, sitting up.

"No, you didn't," said her mother softly. Cora started to cry again.

"You were right," she said between sobs. "He disappointed me. I mean, *he* didn't do it, he was just disappointing. I always thought if he came, I'd recognize him right away. Like I'd know he was my father in some very deep, very . . . I don't know . . ." She wiped her eyes, struggling for words. "I thought we'd fall into one another's arms sort of like in the movies . . . you know, long-lost . . . long-lost . . ." She broke off and hid her face in her mother's lap. Her mother stroked her hair.

"I never thought he'd just show up that way," she said. "*You* were right about that, Cora. You kept saying he would, and then there he was! I almost fainted too."

"You *did* turn very pale," said Cora, looking up and smiling. Her mother smiled back and kissed her lightly on the forehead.

"Butterfly kiss," Cora whispered, hugging her suddenly. "Remember that game? I just thought of it now."

"I can't believe *you* remember it," her mother laughed, shaking her head. "You couldn't have been more than three."

"I'd point to my nose or my chin or even my foot and you'd give me a butterfly kiss wherever I wanted you to, right?"

"Uh-huh. You thought it was very funny." They were quiet for a moment.

"Mom?"

"Hum?"

"It didn't seem as if he remembered that butterfly letter at all. Did it to you?"

"I don't know if he did, sweetie," said her

mother. "Does it really matter?"

Cora stood up and went to the window, pressing her chin to the cool glass. "Yes, it does," she said after a while. Her mother waited, but Cora was silent.

"Do you remember when the elevator in our building was broken?" asked her mother after a while.

"Yes, but what does that have to do . . ."

"Well, when it was out of order it went only to the sixth floor and the basement. If you tried to make it go to any other floor, the car jumped up and down and shook violently, scaring us half to death. And then it would go to the sixth floor or the basement anyway."

"So?"

"So your father is like that elevator, Cora. He can't be any different, no matter what you do or don't do."

Cora laughed.

"You never did eat your pizza; you must be starved," her mother said, laughing too. "Let's have some supper, okay?"

"It's the middle of the night," Cora protested. "Look, there's the moon. What time is it, anyway?"

"It's still early, Cora. But you'd be surprised how many meals I've had in the middle of the night," her mother answered.

Cora turned and studied her thoughtfully. "You know, I've wondered a lot about that lately. I mean, the fact that you never seem to sleep. Like when I saw you making that scrapbook . . ." She paused, not sure why she was bringing all that up now.

"Did it worry you?" her mother asked.

Cora nodded. "I didn't want you to be crazy too," she admitted. "It felt like something I knew about you that I didn't want to, like when I read the letters—something only grown-ups should know."

"Only grown-ups," her mother echoed, and sighed. "I wouldn't have chosen that moment for you to look in on me, Cora," she said. "But I didn't know it worried you so much. I wish you'd told me before."

"Well, I guess you can act strange sometimes and still not be truly off the wall," said Cora. "Right?"

"I hope so," said her mother, smiling.

Cora turned back to the moon. She could see a shadow of her own face in the pane, and she made her shadow eyes wider, staring into them. She remembered how she used to think her dad was living in that glass world, watching her. Well, he had been living in his own parallel place, but he hadn't been watching her. In fact, he didn't know her at all.

Probably they'd always be strangers. Even if she

went to Greece someday to see him when she was older, it wouldn't be like visiting a parent. No, she would never have two parents.

But the thought didn't hurt her as much as it had when she had watched that couple in the park playing with their little boy. She had her mother. And she had Charley. In the moonlight, at least for tonight, that seemed like enough.

"I think if you're really crazy, you can't love anybody the way I love Charley . . . and you," she blurted, not looking at her mother.

"I think that's true," said her mother earnestly.

"You know, Mom, that day I said I was going to the tournament?" she asked, turning and facing her.

"Yes?"

"Well, I was going to go there but I never did. I ended up at Silverpoint—with Charley."

"Okay," said her mother, after a pause. "Is there anything else?"

"No."

"Cora, remember you promised me not to talk to street people anymore, not to interview them with Charley. Are you keeping that promise?"

"No more crazies," said Cora, smiling.

Her mother kissed her lightly on the shoulder. "Let's have some supper," she suggested again.

"Go ahead," said Cora. "I'll come in a few minutes." Her mother exited, and Cora yawned, fingering the two bullet ladies on the windowsill. She clicked them together, then took them in her hand and strolled around the room, absently rolling them like marbles until they grew warm in her palm.

She was too sleepy now to follow her mother into the kitchen, too sleepy to follow her own thoughts.

> *Lady Moon, Lady Moon, where are you roving?*
> *Over the sea, over the sea.*
> *Lady Moon, Lady Moon, who are you loving?*
> *All that love me, that love me.*

She whispered the words to herself, then hummed the tune aloud. Holding the dolls tightly in her hand, she climbed back into bed and stared at the ceiling a moment, as she did every night, counting the shadows of truck windows traveling across the wall and across her father's neckties.

She would keep the ties, and the birdcage and the silly mobile as well. They were hers, after all, as the bullet dolls were hers now. If she and Charley ever parted, she wouldn't part with the dolls the way her mother had parted with all the things that reminded her of Nikos. She would save them, and every time she looked at them, she would think of

Charley, just as he was on the beach that day, after the wave had carried his lamp away.

He had reached down inside his knapsack, pulled out a little piece of string, and deftly fixed her loose shoe. As they walked, the gray in the sky had all gathered into one cloud and the sun had come out, turning the rest of the sky blue.

And then, as simply and miraculously as he had appeared just when she needed him most, he had kissed her.

Cora leaned back on the pillow, letting the sheet slip to her waist, thinking about Charley's kiss. It was swift and brief, like a butterfly landing for an instant on a blade of beach grass. It was solid, like Charley. And it was soothing, like the shadow of a single cloud in a perfectly blue sky.

Cora smiled broadly into the silvery darkness and was instantly asleep. And for the first time since her birthday, she had no dreams at all.